STEALING KARMA

Aneesha Capur has an MFA from Warren Wilson College and an MBA from Wharton. She has attended the Vermont Studio Center, the Bread Loaf Writers' Conference, the Squaw Valley Community of Writers Fiction Program, the Iowa Writers' Summer Workshop, and the Fine Arts Work Center. Her professional career spans private, nonprofit and academic sectors. Aneesha was born in India and spent most of her childhood in Africa. She now lives in San Francisco.

Stealing Karma

Aneesha Capur

HarperCollins *Publishers* India

First published in India in 2011 by
HarperCollins *Publishers* India

Building 10, Tower A, 4th Floor, DLF Cyber City, Phase II,
Gurugram Haryana – 122002, India
www.harpercollins.co.in

ISBN: 978-93-5029-034-7

2 4 6 8 10 9 7 5 3 1

Typeset in Dante MT Std 11/13.7
InoSoft Systems

Printed and bound at
MicroPrints India, New Delhi

For my parents

He looked at his own Soul
with a Telescope. What seemed
all irregular, he saw and
shewed to be beautiful
Constellations; and he added
to the Consciousness hidden
worlds within worlds

Samuel Taylor Coleridge, *Notebooks*

Many lives, Arjuna, you and I have lived,
I remember them all, but thou dost not.

Lord Krishna, *Bhagavad Gita, iv, 5*

PART ONE

Kenya

1

THE AIR WAS QUITE still in the darkened room. The dust shimmered in the sun's rays that slipped through the cracks in the drawn blinds. Mira Sharma breathed in the gold particles that hung suspended around her. She sat up in bed, pulled out her crocheted handkerchief scented with rosewater from the small front pocket of her sweater, and pressed it against her mouth. She stifled a cough. It was an unseasonably warm day for this time of year in Nairobi. Yet Mira was wearing a cashmere sweater over her cotton nightgown.

Prashant Sharma reached across to Mira's side of the bed and hooked his left arm around her hips. The thick curls on his forearm tickled Mira's abdomen. Mira turned towards her husband, trying to extricate herself from him. Prashant tightened his hold on her, his grip became painful. He nuzzled his face into the curve of her waist and began to caress her.

'Prashant, no.' Mira kept her voice low. 'It's time to get up. Shanti must be awake.'

Prashant opened his eyes and looked at his wife. He noticed the patches under her eyes that had made the colour of her face uneven, the creases around her mouth that had crinkled her skin. He wondered at the toll marriage, a child and life on a different continent had exacted on her youth.

'Do you remember the second after I proposed to you, Mira?' Prashant asked her in an effort to lighten her expression and the gravity it had cast over their bedroom. 'The monsoon had just started in Calcutta. We sat on the porch outside your aunt's house, delighting in it while everyone else scuttled indoors. I stared steadfastly into your eyes until you said yes. We got soaked with the warm drops of rain.'

Mira, well-versed in this tactic of disarmament by now, removed her husband's arm from around her body and sat up. She drew up her legs briefly to rest her chin and sighed, letting her feet touch the ground.

Prashant continued, as though Mira's actions were encouragement to further revisit memories of the first moments they had shared together. 'We went out for ice-cream the first time your aunt arranged for us to spend time together. I often think the only reason she so readily agreed to have us marry before you completed your degree at the Loreto Convent was because I sent some kulfi home with you.' He laughed.

Mira switched off the alarm clock on her bedside table, wondering why she ever bothered to set the alarm when every day she awoke hours before it was set to go off. 'Perhaps you should have exported some of it along with your bride from India,' Mira replied, her voice thick.

Prashant leaned across the bed, placing one hand on Mira's shoulder and the other on the back of her head as he turned her towards him. After he had made sure there was no trace of malice on his young wife's face, Prashant said, keeping his tone kind, 'I'll stop by the Indian market in Nagara on my way home and see if the mithai store has made a batch. Their order of cardamom pods arrived from India last week, so they must have some ready by now.'

Mira smiled at Prashant, regretting her lack of generosity moments before. 'You should bring home some of the cardamom and pistachios you import for the stores. Lata said she'd take me to a farm this week in Limuru where they have high-quality milk and cream. And she has some of those conical stainless steel containers which I can borrow and try to make the kulfi at home.'

'I'll bring some from the store,' Prashant said, cupping Mira's face in the palm of his hand. 'You only focus on being happy.' He tapped his index finger against her cheek as he said each word.

Prashant got out of bed and stretched his arms over his head, his fingers almost touching the ceiling. Mira looked at him. Everything about Prashant was enormous: his height, his build, his voice, his laugh. Whenever he stood before her, Mira felt swallowed whole by him. Prashant stopped stretching abruptly. He rubbed his left arm, as if he were trying to massage away a sprain.

'You should spend more time with Lata,' he said to Mira as he walked to the adjoining bathroom. 'We should have her and Mohan over for dinner soon. And it's good for me to build a relationship with a judge as well.'

Wairimu had already given Shanti breakfast by the time Mira and Prashant walked into the dining room. Mira could barely see the top of her daughter's head as she sat by herself at the dining table. The ceramic platters of scrambled eggs and sliced fruit, crystal jugs of orange juice and watermelon juice, silver carafes of coffee and tea laid out on the long mahogany table enveloped the small child. Mira felt guilty that she had left her daughter to eat breakfast on her own, and rushed over to her, covering Shanti's face in kisses.

'Ma!' Shanti said. 'You'll ruin my school uniform.'

'Shanti buckled her own shoes today, but, weh weh, the girl will not let me polish them,' Wairimu said from the doorway leading into the kitchen. Her heavy figure filled the frame, presenting a sturdy image in starched uniform, checkered apron and matching headscarf.

'But the teacher, she said that me, I will learn how to polish my own shoes today in class,' Shanti replied in protest.

'You mean "the teacher told us that I would learn",' Prashant corrected his daughter as he sat at the other end of the table, across from Shanti, and glanced at the newspaper laid by his place setting. 'But what is my daughter doing in a school that teaches its pupils how to polish shoes? We must send you abroad for a proper education.'

'I don't want to go to school with those British bums!'

Shanti quickly covered her face with her hands and peered at her father through her fingers, watching his reaction.

Prashant, astounded by his daughter's proclamation, looked across at Mira who, like Wairimu, had burst into laughter. He kept his glance casual as he registered every detail of this image of Mira before him: her head tilted back as she carelessly shrugged her long hair off her face, letting it spill down her back; her mouth slightly open; her black eyes glittering with humour. Prashant wished he could capture its essence, bottle it and scatter drops around his home every day so he could transform this brief moment of his wife's happiness into something more enduring. He shook his head in silence, finished his cup of tea and stood up.

'Where did you learn to speak this way?' Prashant asked Shanti as he tapped her head with his rolled-up newspaper. 'Go get your books. I'm ready to leave.'

'I won't be home for lunch today,' Prashant told Mira. He leaned down to kiss her cheek. 'I need to see Dr Costa-Correa about this pain in my arm.'

'Prashant.' Mira hesitated, then touched her husband's arm.

'Come straight home this evening, you don't have to go to the store. I don't need kulfi to feel better.'

Prashant smiled at his wife. 'Be well, my dear,' he said; his fingers trailed the part of her face his lips had touched seconds before.

Shanti returned with her school box, a tiny, bright orange suitcase made of cardboard. Prashant took it from her as she stood on her toes to kiss her mother goodbye.

'Ma, let's kiss bye-bye the way you showed me the Eskimos do it,' Shanti whispered as she tried to pull her mother closer.

Mira knelt in front of Shanti and the two rubbed their noses together.

—

As soon as her husband and her daughter had left the house, Mira walked into the kitchen.

'It is good you are not sleeping today,' Wairimu said to Mira, handing her a cup of tea.

'I must call Lata and invite her and Mohan over for dinner this week,' Mira replied.

'Bah. That woman, she talks too much.'

'I know but she's very kind to me,' Mira said, more to give herself, rather than her housekeeper, an explanation. 'Oh, and Wairimu, there's too much dust in the house. Please clean all the bedrooms properly today. Bwana's not coming home for lunch and I'll take care of cooking dinner.'

Wairimu looked surprised at Mira's sudden interest in the housekeeping but said nothing as she left the kitchen, picking up her dustcloth on the way out.

As she sipped her tea, Mira pulled down a recipe book from the top of the fridge and flipped through it. She earmarked a recipe for karhai gosht. Mira took a packet of cubed mutton out of the freezer and left it in the sink to defrost. She then went to the attic to find the two suitcases of her personal belongings that she had brought with her from India. She searched through them until she came across a scrapbook. It was one of a handful of things she still had that belonged to her mother. Mira scanned the pages, searching for a recipe for kheer, the only Indian dessert her mother had made, so she could prepare it for Shanti in the evening. As Mira read her mother's notes written in the margins, intended to enhance each recipe she had pasted into the book, Mira wished Shanti had been able to meet someone who belonged to her family, someone from her past before she became Prashant's wife.

Mira hardly spoke of her childhood so Shanti knew little of it. Mira's parents, Brigadier-General and Mrs K.P. Mistry, were Parsis. Mira's father had served in the British army and then in the Indian army after the country's independence. Her mother published cookbooks filled with recipes of cheese soufflés, caramel custards and jam tarts. They socialized with English officers and their wives. After the British left India, they entertained Indian politicians. Elite, anglicized, infected with madness and depression—the repercussions of an ordinance against conversion and the consequent incidence of inbreeding—the Parsis were a minority group and knew they needed to befriend whoever was in power, whether English, Hindu or Muslim, in order to survive in India. Mira, the Mistrys' only child, was born a year after India's independence. One of Mira's first childhood memories was of her parents waltzing to a tune that was being belted out of the creaking gramophone player in their large living room one afternoon in the middle of the dry Delhi heat. 'Ballroom dancing, my darling, is the greatest gift the British gave us Indians,' Mira's mother had declared as she allowed Mira to squeeze between the soft silk folds of her sari and the starched cotton fabric of Mira's father's trousers. The three of them had continued to dance for the length of the record.

Trying to shake off her memories, Mira made herself focus on the task at hand. She found the recipe for kheer and walked back to the kitchen with her mother's book in her hand. She made a list of the items she would need for dinner and went into the storeroom by the kitchen. She deposited one large onion, a clove of garlic, a stick of ginger, a tub of homemade yoghurt, two cans of sweetened condensed milk, a bag of chopped nuts, a large bottle of corn oil and little plastic packets filled with various spices on the kitchen counter. She walked back to the storeroom and dragged a burlap sack of rice to the kitchen.

The amount of things required to make a simple Indian meal still astonished her. Perhaps because she hadn't been raised around this kind of food. Mira had eaten only English food at home, and when she was eight she had been sent to a Loreto Convent boarding school, where she'd been given the institutional versions of what she'd grown used to at home. Her parents died in a car crash during her first term and the nuns took charge of her. There were two nuns who especially cared for her, Sister Moira and Sister Mary Therese. These women were the first-born daughters of poor Irish families and had joined the Catholic Church. Their vocation was predetermined. India became their home; the Order, their family. They mothered Mira to the point where she hardly grieved for her own parents. She spent her holidays in Delhi with her aunt Erna, a spinster.

Mira leaned against the counter and surveyed each item. Suddenly she felt overrun by the enormity of the task ahead. She wiped away her tears with the sleeve of her sweater and started to measure the ingredients she needed for each dish. She poured out enough cups of rice to eat with the mutton plus the amount she would need for the kheer. She then lugged the sack back to the storeroom. Removing it from the kitchen seemed like a huge accomplishment. Mira rewarded herself by smoking a cigarette, making sure the kitchen window was open so Prashant wouldn't smell the smoke when he returned in the evening. She then emptied the packet of mutton pieces onto a wooden chopping board and trimmed the meat of excess fat. Mira felt uncertain, as if she was playing out an existence whose terms were dictated by someone else. If only she had entered her marriage and had a child out of her own choosing, things would have been different. She wished she were a better mother, a better wife.

Mira was completing her Bachelor's degree at Loreto College in Calcutta when her aunt arranged for her to meet Prashant Sharma. There was an age difference of fifteen years between Mira and Prashant. He had travelled to India from Africa on a business excursion. Prashant was already settled in Nairobi. He owned a lucrative export business here. Sister Moira, Sister Mary Therese and Erna aunty were all pleased with the match. It was a practical marriage, an arrangement that satisfied Mira's guardians since they knew it would open doors to another world for Mira. Prashant Sharma had found an educated Indian bride with a genteel upbringing to care for his home and entertain his guests and, in turn, he offered Mira a life of comfort, security and access to a cosmopolitan world.

Mira peeled and chopped the onion, garlic and ginger. She fried the spices and herbs before adding the mutton and yoghurt. She then washed the rice and cooked two cups in another pot. Mira put the rest of the rice in a pressure cooker and cooked it with milk and sugar. As she timed the preparation of the kheer, she realized it was already midday. While she stirred the milk and rice, she drank the second can of condensed milk to make up for not having eaten anything all morning.

Had it been her first few years here, Mira would have spent the morning sitting at the dining table, pen and paper in hand, a bowl of imported cereal mixed with condensed milk by her side, two treats she paired together that made her feel lavishly indulgent. Mira used to write letters to her two nuns and spinster aunt on the first Monday of every month for three years after she married and moved to Nairobi. All three women died in the same year, when Shanti was two, putting an end to her ritual, and her connection with India. Mira's husband and daughter were now her only family; Africa had become her home.

When the kheer was ready, Mira carefully poured it into a bowl. She lifted the lid of the curry and scooped out a piece of mutton. It needed more time to cook properly. She washed and put away the pressure cooker. She then walked out of the house through the kitchen door.

The Sharmas lived in a bungalow. The house faced a kidney-shaped pool, which was more of a pond really. The pool was surrounded by the kind of garden that would have been an amazing feat to create and maintain elsewhere but was almost effortless in the climate and the soil that existed in Kenya. There was a pepper tree outside the bungalow, two palm trees at the far end of the pool and flame trees opposite. There were hibiscus bushes to the left and clumps of anthuriums, dahlias, lilies and bird of paradise flowers picturesquely strewn all around the finely mowed bright green grass. Roses lined the verandah and there was a small herb garden to one side. All colours of bougainvillea—white, violet, fuchsia, burnt orange—masked the chain-link fence that surrounded the compound. The bungalow had a large patio on the first level that led out to the garden and two small verandahs on the second floor.

Mira sat on a stone ledge in the sun, next to the herb garden, while she waited for the mama mbogas to arrive so she could buy a head of lettuce and a few tomatoes to prepare a salad for dinner.

—

The dust rose in clouds of rust and gold, glinting in the sunshine when it fell from the second floor balcony onto the newly cut lawn below. Wairimu stood up straight, arching backwards to ease the ache in her spine as she waited for the dust to settle. It was already noon and she had only cleaned two carpets. She planned the rest of the day as she brushed off specks of dust from her freshly starched uniform. She would need to change her apron before Bwana Sharma came home but could get away with wiping her blouse and skirt with a damp rag instead of washing her whole outfit again that day.

Taking shortcuts that Mira wouldn't catch was the key to her job. Wairimu quickly smoothed down the tendrils of black wiry hair that were sticking out under her headscarf, as she checked herself in the dressing table mirror in Mira's room through the open balcony door. The dust subsided, leaving a fine red powder on the balcony railing and on her face and clothes. She rolled up the two carpets and carried them back into the bedroom, where she laid them down on either side of the ebony four-poster bed. She patted down the bumps and creases as she lifted each leg of the bed to tuck the ends of the carpet under it.

Someone was ringing the doorbell. Mira's sandals clicked across the floor towards the door. There were women selling vegetables. Mira started bargaining, complaining loudly that one of them had sold her overripe mangoes last week.

'Aiee, aiee! No, mama, no,' the mama mbogas exclaimed, pouted and postured back, calling on the gods to be their witness that they were simple, honest women who didn't have the capacity to even consider selling Mira low-quality goods. 'How can you say such mbaya mbaya things! Me, I am honest. I tell you, my vegetables, they are all sawa.'

Wairimu shook her head as she heard Mira relent and let the mama mbogas set the price for what she was purchasing. Hopefully it was in small quantities, whatever it was, so Wairimu could recoup some of the costs when she bought vegetables in bulk at the market on Saturday.

Wairimu decided to skip dusting Mira's room since she was already running behind her chores and, instead, quickly blew across the row of glass perfume bottles lined up neatly on the dressing table so Mira wouldn't know that the room hadn't been dusted that day.

As she walked out of the room, the housekeeper clicked her tongue disapprovingly at the heavy ebony furniture and carpeting in the room. No wonder Bwana Sharma always complained that the room was hot, Mira's European tastes made it so. Wairimu thought fondly of the last owner she had worked for, the American who had insisted on using African rope beds and leaving the floors bare so she could assimilate herself into the continent. That had suited Wairimu just fine: it meant less dusting and no carpet cleaning. She picked up her still unused dust rag and walked out of Mira's room.

The phone rang, filling the house with its unfamiliar monotone. Mira hurried to the hallway to answer it. Phone calls during the day were rare in the Sharmas' home and always brought about a flutter of activity that disrupted the subdued rhythm that Wairimu and Mira followed when they were alone. Mira wondered who it could be this time. Lata Patel announcing an immediate visit that would set Wairimu and Mira spinning around the house, cleaning, cooking and settling it into a shape of domesticity that wouldn't draw too much criticism from their visitor. Prashant calling to inform her that a business meeting would keep him from coming home for dinner, scuttling Mira's efforts to display to him that she was trying to be a good wife, an active participant in their household. Shanti's school, advising her of some injury or sickness that would bring her daughter home early. Tension stiffened Mira's body at the last possibility and her movements condensed into smaller, slower steps towards the telephone as her muscles weighed into her, heavier with fear.

'Hello?' Mira answered, her voice timid with the lack of familiarity in using the telephone combined with her trepidation at the news it may bear.

'Mrs Sharma?' the voice in the telephone said.

'Yes,' Mira replied, relieved to find it was a stranger at the other end.

'This is Eva, Dr Costa Correa's receptionist.'

'Oh, my husband has an appointment to see the doctor today. You can reach him at the office. Do you have the number?' Mira said, balancing the lettuce and two tomatoes in the crook of her left arm so she could free her right hand to turn the pages of the address book to Prashant's office numbers.

'Mrs Sharma, I'm sorry, it's about your husband,' the woman continued. 'You see, he came here early and Dr Costa Correa wasn't in, so I told him he could wait in the doctor's office. I just went in there to see if he wanted a cup of tea, and he was lying on the couch. I've paged the doctor but it's too late. Mrs Sharma, I'm sorry, he's expired.'

After Mira put down the phone, she realized she had squeezed the tomatoes so hard they had burst open. Bits of red pulp clung to her sweater and dripped onto the open page of the address book, blotting out Prashant's name and office information.

'No, no, what a mess,' Mira whispered desperately, as she tried to brush away the sticky tomato juice from the open page. The damage to the parchment made out of banana fibre was irrevocable. The blue ink of Prashant's tidy handwriting had dissolved, forming smudges across the page.

When Wairimu went downstairs, she found Mira sitting on the floor by the console in the hallway, the head of lettuce still in her hand, the remains of the tomatoes clinging to her sweater and nightgown. Mira was weeping. She carried Mira upstairs, removed her soiled clothes and bathed her. She dressed Mira in a fresh nightgown and put the young woman into bed. She walked back to the hallway and looked up Lata Patel's telephone number in the address book, carefully tracing each letter of the name to make sure she was calling the right person. She opened the top drawer of the console and removed a small key which she used to unlock the dial of the phone. She checked and re-checked every digit before she turned the rotary.

While she waited for Lata to arrive, Wairimu went into the kitchen and threw out the charred remains of the mutton curry. She took a cup of tea up to Mira. Then, as she waited for the woman to arrive who would now give her instructions, who would decide her fate in this household, Wairimu began to dust the furniture.

2

MIRA LOOKED LIKE A miniature doll as she sat at one end of the pyre. At the age of twenty-nine, she could not fathom a life lived alone, without walking two steps behind a husband. Yet she was not young enough to get away with displaying her disbelief, her inability to understand the repercussions of her loss. Unlike Shanti, who fidgeted in an uninterrupted stream of movement by her side, too naïve to realize the stagnant implication of death, Mira affected an everlasting quietude about her. Now, every strand of her thick black hair was combed tidily into a bun at the nape of her neck; the pallu of her white cotton sari was pinned neatly in place against the shoulder seam of her sweater; the makeup was scrubbed off her face; the red vermillion was washed from the narrow straight line of scalp that parted her hair. She sat silently, her fingers linked loosely on her lap, her spine erect. Her eyes rested unwaveringly on the fire in front of her as the flames turned her husband's body into ashes. The women seated by her swayed extravagantly from side to side and expelled gusts of air in whistles and moans, though they had not known her husband well. Mira felt her distaste for them close in.

Mira found that she could not look away from the flames in front of her, the blackness of the burning wood lured her in with a promise of clarity. The void within the fire broke into particles and she saw her journeys through lifetimes as shadows flickered in the flames.

Mira felt a burning sensation race across her body. She wanted to claw at her skin but her mind had lost all command over her physical being. In the flames, she saw a girl run down a small path in a garden, fleeing from the house behind her. In front of the house was a ferocious mob that moved as one body, pulsing with the energy of singular purpose. The mob moved as fast as a forest fire, leaving not one thing in its wake. Mira saw the girl reach a wall at the end of a path. She tried to climb the wall but failed. Sharp stones cut into her arms and legs when she fell to the ground. She tried again and again. The stones ripped her clothes, making deeper gashes into her flesh each time she fell. Behind her the house burned. The mob streamed outwards now, like an army of red ants covering greater areas of earth as their territory widened. The girl finally managed to hurl herself over the wall; her knee bled as she dragged it, scraping over the top.

Mira saw herself standing amidst the remains of a familiar place, burned by hatred. She found herself moving towards familiar walls that were stained a dull ochre. She looked down and saw that she was covered in blood too. She recognized the taste of it. She knew it as well as she knew her own self, her own family. Mira looked around and saw the land surrounding her resolve itself into new crippled and maimed shapes. Shadows moved about her, as though preparing themselves for the next assault. She closed her eyes to fight them away, trying to push herself down into some other, happier place. And then she disappeared inside herself.

Mira opened her eyes, trying to decipher the new image before her. A black shape whirled and turned, revealing and covering flames behind her. A fractious voice screeched at her and she heard a loud pounding. For a moment, Mira thought she was in the path of the dervish and the fire. She tried to duck, crouching away from the approaching impact but she couldn't move. The hooded shape hurtling towards her dissolved when it reached her. She then saw a small body cowering in the flames. The figure was huddled against the earth, as if it was trying to burrow into it. Deep into the fire, Mira saw a crowd descending on the child. She could see their long sticks of bamboo sharpened at one end and fashioned into spears as they were flung into the air and fell on the small body.

Mira tried to speak but could not. Her lips parted hopelessly, her hands lurched forward towards the bleeding child. The dervish came between her and the image. The flames flared into the darkness. Mira could feel the cold of the desert night. The robed woman before her smiled. Her teeth were stained brown and red. There were gaping holes between them. Red rain poured into the desert sand. Mira could no longer see the child. It was as if the earth had opened and swallowed her, taking her away from the terror that reigned above.

Mira felt herself sink into the ground. She opened her mouth to scream, to expunge the horror that she had seen, to expel the image from her body, to clear it from her brain. She heard a shriek. The sound was so harrowing that it cut into her as if she had been stricken. The dervish fled into the darkness and Mira was left on her own. The smell of ash, burnt flesh and charred hair lingered where the flames had been moments ago.

In spite of herself, Mira drew back, stunned. These fragments of memory, of lives that weren't quite her own, fell into place. The seamless nightmares—her daughter's disturbed dreams—took on meaning. Her small mouth formed a perfect oval as a silent stream of grief flowed from her eyes.

Mira looked around her. The dim pyre came into focus once again. She saw the dispersed clumps of grass and bare ground of the cremation field, patches of grass were bright in the light shining from behind the clouds covering the sky. The air was filled with smoke. The funeral was over. She stood up and shook off the soot that had collected in her sari. Shanti imitated her, trying to mirror every movement her mother made. Without looking at her, Mira took Shanti's hand into her own. The pair walked back into the temple in silence, their shadows outlined by the sun in the doorframe, a perfect silhouette of grief, a widow and her daughter.

—

Mira and Shanti weren't left on their own for the rest of the day. The Patels drove them home. Lata had brought food with her, it was already laid out on the dining table waiting for them.

'We should serve some meat,' Mira said as she looked at the dishes. Rice and dal had been prepared with no spices. Grains of semolina soaked in milk were divided into small bowls. 'Prashant liked to eat meat.'

'Don't be silly, dear,' Lata said to Mira as she steered her into the living room. 'That's not our custom.'

Lata made Mira and Shanti sit on a cotton rug that was spread out on the living-room floor and wait for the guests. Visitors, people who Mira didn't know, streamed into the house through the afternoon. They left their shoes by the door, they offered condolences and brought food. Mira sat in silence, her eyes cast downward, still holding Shanti's hand in her own. The women from the funeral joined them on the floor. They patted Shanti's head and murmured their sympathies to Mira, expecting neither of them to respond. Shanti sat silently by her mother's side, watching her mother weep. She was her consoler, her helper, her shadow.

For three days and three nights, Mira and Shanti were made to sit and sleep on the ground. They received guests through the day and night. Lata brought the same food every day, which they shared in the evening, amongst themselves and with whoever had stopped by at that time. On the third night, after most of the visitors had left, Lata and some of the other women helped Mira up, raising her from her position on the floor. She took a bath, shedding the white sari she had been wearing since the funeral.

Mira emerged from her bedroom to find that the only guests who remained were Lata and Mohan Patel. Her mourning period was officially over. She was now left unaided in her house, to begin her new existence as a widow.

When Mira went downstairs, Shanti ran to her, attaching herself to her mother once more. Lata and Mohan sat in the living room, opposite Mira.

'Shanti, you must need to go to the bathroom,' Lata said. 'You're excused.'

Shanti looked up at her mother expectantly. Mira reluctantly let go of her hand.

'Mohan and I want to talk to you about your plans. You must want to leave as soon as possible.'

'Leave?' Mira raised her eyes to the couple seated before her. 'But I have nowhere to go. This is my home now.'

'Mira, this is no place for a young woman to raise a child on her own,' Mohan interjected, glancing anxiously at his wife. 'Besides, there must be someone in India who you can go to.'

'There's no one,' Mira said. 'There's only me, Shanti and Wairimu.'

'Wairimu is a servant,' said Lata.

Mohan placed a hand on his wife. 'I don't think you understand the implications of remaining here.' He paused, as though to make sure he was articulating clearly to the young widow. 'Things are changing. There'll be some political unrest, for sure.'

'Prashant has family, I'm certain, in Canada,' Lata said, interrupting Mohan.

'I'm not going to live with in-laws,' said Mira. She stared at them, resolute, defying a response.

After a moment, Mohan slapped his palms on his knees. 'Well, it's settled then,' he said and stood up, leaving Lata no choice but to follow his lead. 'I'll ask Prashant's lawyer, David Silverstein, to stop by tomorrow to speak to you about executing his will.'

Lata opened her mouth to speak but Mohan raised his hand to silence her. 'And you will remain here if that's what you've decided,' he said, ending the discussion.

Wairimu and Shanti were sitting together at the dining table, mugs of tea in their hands. Mira joined them, ladling herself some tea from the large sufuria on the stove in the kitchen. It struck her that she hadn't seen Wairimu since the day of the funeral, and that the housekeeper wouldn't have dared sit at the dining table if Prashant, or even Lata, were here. Mira took a sip of the hot, sweet tea and then stood up to get a coaster from the dashboard and carefully placed her mug on it. Wairimu and Shanti snatched up their mugs, quickly wiping away with their bare hands the rings of condensation on the polished wood surface. Mira decided to ignore them while they furtively dried their hands under the table, Wairimu on her apron and Shanti on one of the few unsoiled dresses she had that Lata had made her wear.

'That woman, she made me stay in the kitchen. Me, I wasn't even allowed to touch all that food she brought with her,' Wairimu told Mira.

'And me, I was made to sit on the rug all day and not allowed to go outside to play,' Shanti said, her expression and voice a carbon copy of the housekeeper's, their defining lines lighter and blurred, more easily erased and transformed into something else.

Mira looked first at Wairimu and then at Shanti. The two, in response, fidgeted uncomfortably in silence.

'Well,' said Mira, deliberately. 'You must realize it wasn't any picnic for me either.'

Wairimu turned to Shanti for an explanation but the little girl only mimicked the housekeeper's puzzled stare.

'You silly geese!' Mira said. 'Do you really think I liked Lata breathing down my neck all day, telling me what to do and pointing out everything I did wrong?'

The three of them burst out laughing. Wairimu slapped her thighs, the table and Shanti's back. Shanti fell out of her chair and onto the carpet, rolling around on her back, her hands and legs in the air.

'Heh, Shanti. You look like an ant who has been turned upside down on its back,' Wairimu said, patting the sweat on her forehead with her apron.

'Yes, an ant that's showing the world her underpants,' Mira said, wiping tears from her eyes. She reached down and grabbed Shanti's arms, pulling her into her lap.

'Hey, ma, I want to stay down here,' Shanti objected.

'What? Haven't you had enough of moping about on the floor?' Mira raised her eyebrows at Shanti as she settled her daughter into her lap. Shanti responded by raising her eyebrows as well.

'Sasa,' Wairimu said, laying her palms on the table. 'Now tell me, what does that woman want you to do?'

'I think you know,' Mira replied. She took out a pack of cigarettes and a box of matches from the pocket of her nightgown. Her fingers shook as she lit her cigarette, in the open. She had no one to hide her smoking from now. 'Sell the house, pack up and leave as soon as possible.'

'And it is to be?'

'No, Wairimu, it is not to be, so you can take that forlorn look off your face.' Mira held up her hand to stop Wairimu from responding. 'We're staying.'

'Yay!' Shanti shouted. She slid off Mira's lap and put a coaster on top of her head. She balanced her empty mug on the coaster and started swaying around the room, bobbing her neck up and down.

'Shanti, I tell you,' Wairimu laughed. 'You could be a Mwa-Afrikan!'

'Well, she isn't, and neither am I,' Mira said to Wairimu. 'And Mohan said that we should leave because of that.'

'Tcha!' Wairimu responded, dismissing both Patels with a sweep of her hand.

'He has a point, Wairimu,' Mira said. 'He says things are getting bad here politically, and that we Indians will pay for it.'

'It is not Indians like you, Mira,' Wairimu replied. 'It is the muhindis, the ones that have been here for too many years and think they are so much better than us.'

'And will they know the difference when they come to slaughter us in our homes?'

'I will be here to tell them.'

'Wairimu, they'll kill you too.'

'You keep your trust in me,' Wairimu said. 'No harm will come to this baby who is of your womb and of my land.'

Wairimu reached across the table and took both Mira's hands in her own while Shanti continued to dance amidst the hazy serrations of cigarette smoke that had filled the entire room.

'Shanti, come with me,' Mira woke her daughter, pulling her out of bed. 'It's a full moon.'

They walked barefoot to the garden, their bodies covered only by the thin cotton of their nighties. Mira ran ahead of her daughter into the cool air under the African hibiscus trees. Shanti remained on the patio, afraid of the night, incandescent in the moonlight. She lost sight of Mira and felt a ripple of panic. Her fear of the shadowy night surrounding her disappeared. She tried to catch up with her mother, but she failed and doubled over with a stitch in her left side. She sat on the ground as she felt the pain had become too much to bear standing upright.

'I give up,' Shanti shouted out in between gasps. 'Come back, mama. You win, again.'

Mira returned from the shadows at the bottom of the garden. She reached for Shanti and pulled the little girl alongside her with one fluid motion. Shanti let her mother's easy energy wash over her. As Mira dragged Shanti towards her favorite spot in the garden, the water hose by the bottlebrush tree, Shanti protested, laughing, raising her arms over her face in mock resistance, but Mira stooped down and sprayed kisses on her mouth, her cheeks, her eyes, her neck, until Shanti said she wasn't scared any more and agreed to race down the length of the garden with her.

Later that night, Shanti had a dream. She was a small girl of about five years. She was wearing a blue and white pinafore, a school uniform perhaps. She wore a pair of black leather shoes with silver buckles. Her hair was parted to one side and pulled back from her face with a small clip. She came home from school to her house, which had a huge porch and a garden. She found it empty. Everything in the house was gone: the carpets, the furniture, even the fans that hung from the ceiling. She ran to her room, which had also been stripped bare. She searched frantically for her doll but couldn't find her. Then she heard footsteps in the corridor and a shadow entered her room. She sensed that it was her mother. 'Keya, you have to go now,' her mother breathed. The woman took her by the hand and led her outdoors, making her sit by a wall on the side of the road. Time passed. Slowly the air surrounding her turned into dust and blood. She was petrified. She could do nothing but sit and wait as a cloud of murky red settled over her.

Shanti woke abruptly from the nightmare and found herself alone in her mother's bed. She walked into the corridor and saw Mira sitting on the ground, her back towards the bedroom door. Mira's knees were pulled towards her chest, her arms were locked around herself. Shanti held her mother as she wept.

'Don't worry, mama. I'll take care of you,' Shanti whispered into Mira's ear.

'Keya, Keya, Keya,' Mira moaned softly, as if she were singing a lullaby.

'It'll be okay, ma. I promise,' Shanti said, desperate for her mother to stop crying, knowing now, upon hearing that name, that her mother was seconds away from falling into a confusing abyss of darkness where she would remain for days at a time.

Mira turned to Shanti and kissed her. It was a sweet, lingering kiss. And even though Shanti was wide awake by now and had successfully conquered the demons that had chased her into her dream world, she didn't resist when her mother lifted her and carried her back to bed.

3

A SENSE OF FREEDOM filled the Sharmas' home after the mourning period for Prashant ended. Shanti didn't hear anyone mention the loss of her father. Wairimu stopped wearing her uniform the day after Lata and the other mourners left the house. Shanti knew Mira had noticed but chose not to mind. Shanti liked to see the bright colours Wairimu draped over herself. Wairimu's body was a warm ebony and she wore all the colours of a peacock—crescent sheens of ultramarine and imperial green—a dazzling spectacle as she sat outside the house in the sun, plaiting her hair. This was the first time Shanti had seen Wairimu's head uncovered. She usually wrapped her head in a scarf that matched her uniform. Wairimu had stopped cleaning the house every day and hardly washed the clothes or cooked. Instead, she stretched out her long, muscular body in the sun, spending her days chatting with the gardener or the night watchman and playing in the garden with Shanti. After all, she only had one person to cater to now, and Shanti preferred to eat ugali and sukuma wiki, the maize meal and spinach Wairimu made for herself over her charcoal stove in the courtyard outside her quarters.

This veiled sense of abandon permeated Mira's existence as well. For the first time in her life, Mira had no one to whom she had to answer, no one to whom she had to give an account of her whereabouts. Mira felt like a young moth that had suddenly discovered the night, trailing smoke and shadow as it began its first ascension. She ventured out, tentatively at first, discovering a new city and a new self. And then she immersed herself in her newly forged freedom, swooping high and low, manoeuvering through her new life with incredible ease, as if she didn't have a care in the world.

Mira stopped spending time with Lata, or anyone who knew Prashant, and started to explore the city. She was out most days and nights, going on her own to shops, galleries, museums, restaurants, bars. She came back to sleep in her bed, only as a result of Wairimu's concern that if she didn't return every night it would look bad to the neighbours and their servants, and also because of her own desire to return to Shanti so she could hold her close and feel as if she'd contributed her daily quota of love. As Mira drove into their fenced-in home each night, she could sense Wairimu and Shanti waiting, peering out from the verandah into the dimly lit grounds beneath, watching for her return. They were a pair, a unit, her small family. When Mira turned the key in the front door, she heard them quickly leave their positions and settle into some place where she might believe them to be asleep, or at least not waiting up for her.

—

A few months later, another man entered Mira's life, leaving everyone to wonder where the young widow had learned to be so intrepid. Truth be told, their wonder was justified. Mira did not have the background or the education that encouraged libertine relationships. She had neither read the kinds of books nor met the kinds of people that might have lured her in that direction. She just became that sort of woman, like a chameleon twisting around to fit into its newly hatched existence after managing to pull off an old skin.

'Oh, the guile of the girl!'

'And so soon after her husband's death!'

'Not to mention the low quality of her choice—his class, his colour, his creed, his culture.'

The other women hissed absurdly as they withdrew into the comfort of each other's company, fortifying their Brahmin-based, Indo-Anglophile prejudices. What they didn't realize as they stewed in this outrage to their own sensibilities was that Mira, rather than indulging a streak of obstinate recklessness, was accommodating the first person who sought her out, as if she had no choice in the matter. Mira was frightened of being alone. Her whole life, she had battled against herself. A self that possessed the silent resignation that she would not be able to, on her own, save herself or her daughter from the dull-thud sense of destruction that resided at the edges of her existence, waiting to take over. But this new reptilian self that existed with the absence of remembering grief kept the hope that the present had to be more a promise of what lay ahead than a haunting of the past. Her fault, due to her still youthful wishes and desires, lay in the placement of this self on the will of men for its survival and, in some measure, in the strand of impudent daring that had always existed in her but was only now allowed to surface. Despite the indoctrination of others, Mira couldn't cultivate their discriminations, especially given the precariousness of her own position in the past.

—

Toby was different from any of the other uncles Shanti knew. He seemed much older than her mother. He always wore a black turban and long, undulating robes. His hair was a mass of braids, the colour of steel, with tiny bright glass beads plaited into the ends. They spilled out of his turban onto his shoulders and down his back. His eyes frightened Shanti. The whites were bright, each forming a luminous pond upon which floated a small black marble. A thin moss of wiry grey curls covered his chin. Shanti couldn't see much of the rest of his body. Toby's figure was always silhouetted in his black cotton robes. He wore leather thongs on his feet, regardless of the weather. Shanti couldn't help but admire his jewellery: strands of beads of different lengths adorned his chest; some mirrored the glinting ones in his hair, others were carved out of wood to match the beads dangling from his ears and toes. He spoke in an American accent which didn't seem to fit his wardrobe at all. He carried a Q'uran and a prayer mat wherever he went, and stopped whatever he was doing five times a day to unroll his mat on the floor, open his book and kneel to pray.

Toby was an American who had converted to Islam. Under Sharia law, he allowed himself multiple wives. His first wife was an American photographer with whom he had travelled to Africa. They lived with nomads across sub-Saharan Africa so she could take pictures of them that were displayed in large glossy books that lay on people's coffee tables in Nairobi and, the Sharmas imagined, in other metropolitan areas around the world.

His second wife was a nomadic girl from Niger. For their wedding ceremony, Toby adorned himself in the robes the men wore every day to protect themselves from the desert wind and sand. As soon as he had put on the clothes and looked at his reflection, he decided this would be his daily attire from then on. His first wife had participated in the wedding, dancing under the desert sky. She had taken photographs of her husband and his new bride that were later featured in her coffee-table books as authentic tribal rituals.

His third wife was a Kenyan woman. Through his marriages, Toby had assured himself access to the countries where he desired residence: the United States (where, the Sharmas learned, he had been convicted for a crime and would be arrested upon arrival if he travelled under his original identity), Niger (where he could live, temporarily, the existence of a desert nomad) and Kenya (a go-between of sorts, a place to transit between his other lives).

Toby was with his first wife when he met Mira and Shanti. Despite Lata's reproof that it was too soon after Prashant's funeral, Mira had decided to show the roses she had grown in her garden at an annual flower exhibition.

The Sharmas were out of place there. The only other Indian was the wife of a prominent Indian industrialist who didn't recognize Mira without Prashant. Her flowers took over one entire side of the main tent. The woman's prize collection, and assured winner of the exhibition, was her display of orchids. Her husband had built a state-of-the-art greenhouse for her in their garden which was as big as the Sharmas' house, and their house itself was the size of an English mansion. The woman's and her flowers' presence were both considered to be acts of charity, a token gesture to support cultural activities in Kenya, though no one seemed to recognize that the culture belonged to a colonial heritage. Every year, her eye was set on the real prize, at an international orchid conference somewhere else in the world. She'd flown her orchids into Durban last year where she was placed first at the World Orchid Conference.

Former colonialists' wives took up most of the rest of the hall. Skinny old British women sporting heavy eye shadow, dangling earrings and strange clothing—silk scarves knotted around their heads, flapper dresses and old stockings to cover varicose veins draped loosely over the rest of their bodies—utterly inappropriate for this place and this time. They had brought flowers from their farms upcountry. Younger English women, dressed in riding clothes, though there weren't any horses around, showed flowers from their gardens in Karen, still a predominantly white residential area on the outskirts of Nairobi. Few actual residents of the city had come to see the exhibition. People who were willing to pay the entrance fee were either expats or tourists, believing this to be another event to round out their African experience. All of it, the exhibition and the people involved, were relics of an age that was over.

Toby and his wife were the only ones who bothered to stop at Mira's stall. Shanti spent the entire time watching Toby's wife in fascination while she admired Mira's roses and exclaimed over and over that they were just gorgeous. The woman asked if she could take photographs of the two Sharmas along with their, to be perfectly frank, paltry display of flowers.

Shanti then watched, with a growing sense of alarm, as this odd, robed man walked behind the table where her mother was standing and tried to stick one of her flowers, which he had just killed by snapping its stalk, into her hair and succeeded in ruffling her neat chignon in the process.

Her anxiety never subsided in the following weeks, as Toby transformed from a stranger, just another man among a throng of men in the public spaces that she occasionally had to visit, into her mother's friend, one who felt entitled to disrupt the haven of domesticity they had inhabited since her father's death.

Not long after he entered their lives, Toby made Shanti and Mira breakfast one Sunday morning. It was Wairimu's day off, and he was already in the kitchen, wearing his usual desert garb, when Shanti woke up and made her way there.

She joined her mother at the table. They sat and watched with an equable curiosity as he poured maple syrup—which he had brought with him all the way from America and introduced into their kitchen—over three stacks of pancakes. When he served Mira, Toby murmured that he was thinking of taking an Indian bride for his fourth wife. Shanti hated pancakes with maple syrup, and Toby, from that instant, while she watched her mother look at him archly, flutter her eyelashes and let out a teasing gurgle of laughter.

That morning, as Shanti forced herself to eat the pancakes, which now tasted like they were made of papier mache and then soaked in a vomit-inducing, sweet, viscous liquid, Toby told Mira he had killed a man when he was nineteen.

'I shot him on the corner of 127th and Broadway in the plain light of day. It's what you did then to get by. I needed cash. I hadn't embraced the word of god yet. In prison, Prophet Muhammad, peace be upon him, came to me. I tried changing my way of life when I got out. But the law don't make it easy for you to change. That's why I left and came here.'

Mira was sympathetic. This woman, who was usually so calm and unruffled among her husband's associates, the only other men Shanti had seen her with, seemed enraptured by Toby's story. With her face flushed and her voice breathless, Mira told him she understood and, to Shanti's utter amazement, said she had, in the past, made similar, difficult decisions herself.

'Our circumstances force us to do things we wouldn't even dream of normally,' Mira told Toby. 'Believe me, I've done things I'm not proud of, things I can't even bear to think of. I know what it's like.'

Shanti couldn't believe, no matter how hard she tried or how much she enjoyed imagining, her mother standing at a street corner in New York City, wearing a trench coat and a hat over her sari, a cigarette dangling from her lips, her face masked by a shadow, as she raised a revolver and shot a person in the swirling fog under the murky yellow beam of a street light.

Shanti wasn't the only one in the household who disapproved of Toby. Wairimu sulked whenever he came to the house. She refused to serve him anything, claiming she had more important chores that required her attention. In order to avert a domestic dispute, Mira pretended that she preferred to attend to Toby herself and made him tea or cooked for him herself, if she knew beforehand that he would be stopping by.

'And what kind of a man is that one who doesn't even have a surname?' Wairimu said to Shanti one afternoon in the kitchen when Toby was visiting and Mira had sent her in to get them some water to drink.

'A surname?' Shanti repeated in astonishment, since she'd never thought of grown-ups having proper names before.

'Yes, it is so. Go ask him if you want. Me, I have heard from the other maids that he does not like to give his name to the mamas he makes friends with. And then he disappears, like the wind. He is very shifty, I tell you.'

'Uncle Toby,' Shanti said in her most innocent voice when she returned to her mother and him, carefully setting the tray with two glasses and an old bottle of Johnnie Walker Red Label now filled with water on the table. When Shanti unscrewed the cap, a faint scent of whiskey along with the memory of her father escaped from the bottle. 'What's your surname?'

'Really, darling,' Mira said quickly, in embarrassment. 'What kind of a question is that? Don't mind her, Toby.'

They tried to laugh off Shanti's question, but Shanti would have none of it. She stood in front of Toby, placed her hands on her hips and said, 'Please, sir. Wairimu and I demand to know what your full name is. You have ours. It's only fair you give us yours.'

Toby kept laughing but Shanti could see his eyes harden and his lips thin. She thought she spied him surreptitiously curling his fingers into a fist and worried that he would find her later, when she was alone, and pound her skin until it looked like one of the cowhides that were sold in the open-air market that Wairimu took her to on the first Saturday of every month.

'Toe—Bee. See, you can make two names out of what you already got. Does that satisfy you, girl?'

Mira laughed nervously and steered Shanti firmly by her shoulders, out of the room, before she had a chance to think up a clever response. Shanti was forced to return empty-handed to Wairimu, who clicked her tongue against her teeth several times when she was told how Toby and Mira had responded.

Shanti came home from school one afternoon to find Wairimu waiting for her outside the front door.

'Come quickly, hurry up,' the housekeeper said, ushering Shanti into the kitchen.

'Wairimu, what's wrong?' Shanti asked, suddenly frightened, remembering the day she had been told that her father was dead.

'Weh, that bad man is with your mother again,' Wairimu whispered as she tied and untied the front of her skirt into knots. 'Go in there and do something.' She pushed Shanti into the hallway, barely allowing her time to put down her small suitcase of books.

Shanti walked into a thick cloud of smoke, the smell of sweet cloves. She could hear the rhythms of different drumbeats from the living room. Shanti had just been taught what Zairean music was, in a class at school, and was surprised to learn that her mother owned a record of African music. When she peered into the room, she saw Mira sitting on the sofa, her hair let down. Her mother's sari had been hoisted up to reveal her slender legs, her feet were bare except for a pale pink varnish that covered her toes. Shanti felt shock wash over her as she stared at this casually intimate picture of her mother, a sight usually only reserved for her daughter. Toby was sitting very close to Mira.

'Just like a little bird,' he was saying to her as he leaned in, 'Mira, you're my little bird.'

Shanti heard a noise. It was high-pitched. It was coming from her. Shanti found her mouth straining to open wider and wider, her eyes strained wide open too.

'La la la la la la la,' she chanted as she ran towards them.

She collapsed at her mother's feet.

'I can make this kind of music too. I learned it in school,' Shanti whispered to her mother, her voice barely audible.

The cup Mira was holding clattered against its saucer as she spilled tea all over her lap.

'Oh dear,' she said, scrambling to stand up as she patted down her sari and dropped tea on Toby in the process.

Shanti could feel Toby's glare as he got up to wipe his robes and appear concerned over Mira spilling tea on herself. Shanti was not sure of what to do next. Exhausted, she picked herself off the floor. She twirled a few times in the middle of the carpet and then la-la-ed her way back to the hallway and into Wairimu's arms.

None of them saw or spoke of Toby after that afternoon.

4

TOBY'S ABRUPT DEPARTURE FROM the Sharma household was barely registered as a cascade of events turned their lives upside down, to an extent that they could never be restored to their original balance. On the first day of August, during the same week that Toby disappeared, there was a failed coup attempt by the Kenyan Air Force. The president, Daniel Arap Moi, took a hard line against any opposition, sniffing out members of his government who may have collaborated to oust him, and crushed them. He then let his police force reign free. They raided people's homes under the pretence of national security. They were brutal. Civilians offered them bribes in exchange for protection. The policemen took their payoffs obligingly, and then proceeded to pillage their property anyway.

Kenyans of Indian origin were especially a target for violence. The immigrant population was the merchant class in the economy and was often used as a scapegoat by the government, who pointed to their success as a group as the reason why the rest of the nation had failed. Any Kenyan Asian family was fair game, not black enough to be recognized as kin, not white enough to admire. All Indians were to be blamed and punished for any negative feeling an African might experience, which ranged from something as trivial as having a bad day to being the victim of prejudice that many Kenyan Asians displayed to black Africans. A large portion of the Indian immigrant class thought they were superior to Africans. They worked hard, toiling away at their trade in a country they disregarded as they accumulated and stored their wealth abroad. Most Kenyan Asian families held a ticket out of this place, usually a foreign passport that offered them a right of abode in England or Canada. They too cast their nets towards the whiter, western landscape for the future, looking down on the continent to which they now belonged and on the land of their origin.

Mira's late husband's assets were frozen during this time. He had been linked to a prominent African lawyer who was involved in the failed coup. An enquiry was being held against the lawyer. All his associates had fled the country, liquidating their wealth before their retreat into anonymity.

Mira found herself left on her own, in a land where she did not belong, with no income and a daughter to support in the swirl of this turmoil. She knew there would be no distinction made between herself, a foreigner who happened to live here by way of an arranged marriage, and the Indian immigrant class that was fast becoming the sole object for mass hostility as other, whiter races evacuated the land.

Mira stayed in her house while everyone else she knew either left or paid exorbitant sums of money to have their homes made more secure. Higher walls were constructed, the tops of which were covered with electrified wire and spikes of glass. Private armies were hired, personal guards strutted upon secure properties, brandishing weapons. Mira had inherited the house from her husband and couldn't afford to move out or do anything to bar easy admission to it, since she no longer had access to Prashant's bank accounts. Through the town auction, she sold most of the furniture and their possessions, keeping only a few items of jewellery and clothes as tokens of her former existence. Although she didn't attend, she learned from Lata that people she knew, people who Prashant had counted among his friends, had been there, raising their paddles, striving to acquire his things even as they disassociated themselves from her. Mira had to let the gardener go who used to come every second day to help her with weeding and mowing. She terminated the contract with the driver from Prashant's trading business who came by to take Shanti to school during the week. That was all the help she had, except for Wairimu, who she kept on by paying her small installments from the money she had acquired from the fire sale.

Mira found that her status had been transformed overnight, by a political action from which she was far removed and had neither any knowledge of nor any proclivity towards. She had fully become the kind of person that most of the people she knew now refused to associate with so they could protect their own status, their wealth, their position in the political and social pecking order of the country's regime.

Starlings flew over the house and settled on the flame trees in the garden. Some scattered into the empty pool to peck at the broken tiles, chipping away at the lining of the ceramic basin. A gunshot perforated the air and the birds fluttered back to the trees, only cautiously returning after moments of silence.

Mira sat at the kitchen table. Her body jerked whenever she heard a bullet explode into the sky. Wairimu stood against the sink and watched Shanti play in the garden.

'You should call her in,' Mira said. 'It's almost time for the curfew.'

'Is it already seven? I have to walk to the duka. We need milk.'

'Forget it,' Mira said. 'We'll go shopping tomorrow. It's too dangerous to go now.'

'Tcha!' Wairimu replied. She started looking for her slippers.

'Wairimu, it's true. I spoke to Lata today and she said Bobby Singh—remember the turbaned man who came with his blonde English wife when Prashant called people over for dinner last year?—he was driving with his wife in town last week and they got caught after the curfew. The police had made a roadblock to check all the cars. They didn't want to stay in the traffic so he reversed, thinking he'd drive through Langata instead to get home, and the police shot at the car. A bullet hit his wife and killed her instantly.'

'Polé. Sorry for her death. But that's the problem with you muhindis and mzungus. You think you are special. You think you are above our law.' Wairimu put her slippers away near the kitchen door and returned to her position by the sink.

'And what laws are these that Africans can come into our homes and take anything they want? Lata said they are raping Indian girls, as young as ten years old. What law says that is all right?' Mira placed her head on the table, letting her forehead rest against the cool surface.

'That is not what I am saying. Sawa, there are bad men out there for sure.'

'Well, if they come here, I want you to take Shanti into your quarters and stay there, okay? No matter what happens. No matter what they do to me.'

'I tell you we need an askari here, however old he is, just to show we are protected. Did you ask that woman?'

'Yes, I did.' Mira paused, keeping her head on the table, her eyes closed. 'Lata said if she sent someone it would show that she is against the president. She said she can't risk it.'

'And why would the president care what she does? Weh, weh. That woman thinks she is too important.'

'Well, I suppose Mohan is one of the few political appointments who is muhindi.'

'And so he will do the old man's dirty work.'

'Shush, Wairimu. We can't speak like that. Someone might hear.' Mira raised her head from the table and looked around as if she expected the president to walk out of the shadows in the corners of her kitchen.

'So you think there is a man standing on the porch, listening to what we are saying?' Wairimu folded her arms across her chest, getting ready to face off with an intruder in the house.

'I don't know,' said Mira. She walked to the sink and drew the curtains across the kitchen window. 'I'm frightened.'

Two headlights throwing lines of yellow chemical light marked the way to the Sharmas' house. As the sound of boots descending from the land rover onto the gravel driveway recoiled into their bedrooms, Wairimu ran from her quarters through the kitchen door, up the stairs to Shanti's room. Mira, who had got there before her, was wild-eyed and lost in the inauguration of an attack. She held onto Shanti, keeping one hand pressed tightly over her daughter's mouth. Wairimu pulled Shanti from Mira's arms.

They heard a loud rapping noise on the front door. Wairimu covered Shanti in a kanga, gathering the ends of the material in each hand and lifting the girl onto her back. She slung one end of the kanga over her left shoulder and brought the other end around her waist under her right arm, tying the material into a knot at the front of her body, underneath her chin. She ran out of the house, through the kitchen door, carrying Shanti, who wrapped her arms and legs around the housekeeper's neck and waist.

Two men, holding rifles and dressed in khaki shorts and caps, barred the front door. Mira recognized their police uniforms. Without speaking, she let them in. A man in a grey suit entered the house after them.

'Mrs Sharma,' he said to Mira, extending his right hand. 'Let me introduce myself. I am Francis Gichuku.'

Mira, helpless in her bewilderment, took his hand. The man saw the lack of recognition in her eyes. His face turned harder, he strengthened his grip on her hand.

'I am the meen-ist-ah of ed-you-ca-shon.' The man spat out the title at her, emphasizing each syllable as if he was shouting through a loudspeaker to a cheering crowd in Nairobi stadium.

Mira shrank a little but tried not to pull away from his grasp. 'Would you like some tea?' Her voice leaked out in sharp spurts, revealing her fear.

'Yes,' the minister replied, letting go of her hand. He nodded in approval at her gesture of hospitality. She had shown him the requisite measure of respect.

'Go make us tea,' he ordered. 'We will have a look around your house.'

In the kitchen, Mira set her teeth together to stop herself from shaking. She filled the kettle and lit the stove. Mira fumbled as she took out her best china from the glass cabinet in the dining room. The fragile ceramic shattered as soon as it grazed the surface of the wooden floor, the noise matched the crunch of boots above as the three men scoured every room. Mira jumped back, alarmed at the mess she had made. She hit the corner of the dining table. She thought it was a rifle butt and screamed. At that instant the kettle started to whistle. Mira turned around and backed away, walking into the scattered pieces of the teacups. The splinters cut into the soles of her feet, the gashes filled with blood.

The men returned downstairs.

'We will not stay,' declared the minister. 'We have seen enough.'

His lips curled as his eyes swept over Mira, taking in her bare feet in a pile of broken china, the rest of her barely covered in a cotton nightie. Her vulnerability seemed too intense, too easy almost, and he looked away.

'You should keep your house in better condition,' he said, turning to leave.

'Why?' Mira asked, startled at her own bravado, wishing she had censured herself.

'Because,' the minister replied, not bothering to look back as he walked away, 'I might want it for myself one day.'

One of the policemen tapped his partner on the shoulder, pointing at the shattered china with his rifle before they followed the minister out of the house. He looked at Mira and grinned, revelling in the evidence of her terror. Almost as an afterthought, the other policeman swept his hand across the remaining tea setting Mira had laid out on the table and laughed as the cups and saucers smashed to the floor.

5

THEIR TWO HEADS WERE bowed over the shards of glazed clay strewn across the hardwood floor. They were kneeling in silence, as if in prayer, as they collected each piece and placed it on a tray, gluing the broken china to form a baroque mosaic. Mira began to hum, swaying a little as she shaped a prism of detail with the miniscule broken parts. Shanti clapped, marvelling at the design which reflected the spare light arching through the window and fashioned colourful patterns as shadows scaled the walls of the dining room. She put her arms around her mother's neck. Mira stopped collecting the fragments of china and closed her hands around Shanti's chubby fingers. They stayed like that for minutes as Mira rocked Shanti. They hugged and stroked, diving into and drinking in one another. This was, this ought to be, where they belonged. They should not, either of them, have had to part.

'I hope Wairimu likes the gift we're making her,' Shanti said, burrowing her face into her mother's neck.

'She will,' Mira murmured in reply. 'And we'll turn the beastly fortune of broken clay in our house into something beautiful.'

'Or into a beautiful beast!' Shanti giggled.

Mira, still rocking Shanti, turned her head slightly, away from the window. Her eyes turned to the dark house.

She heard fists on the door from another time. The city was enveloped in a shroud of black, suffering from power cuts for the third consecutive week. The low light from her kerosene lamp guided her to the front door. She took the iron key from the ring tied to the end of her sari, unlocked the padlock and unwound the links of chain so she could slide open the heavy wooden door to let in the night.

'Look, Shobha ma,' the girl whimpered. 'See what they have done.'

The girl's salwar kameez was soiled and torn in the most menacing places. Dull brown stains spread over her top and the wet fabric clung to her chest, outlining each breast. Bruises marked her face, her neck, the places where her flesh was exposed.

The shopkeeper, the gardener, the butcher, the butcher's son, familiar faces, the substratum of communal living, fused together to form a marauding cavalry, nameless, faceless, joined in the name of a discriminating god. They lowered their eyes in his honour. And when they raised their heads again, they could see nothing but their own hate.

They recited the Kalma as they played their own versions of god in the servant quarters of the British Indian army cantonment areas, land that, in the blink of an eye, would become Pakistan. They selected among the young girls, who would die, who would suffer a fate worse than death, ravaged, spoiled, left over, shunned by her own people and her own religion, and who would be merely teased, exposed, touched, threatened by their careless intimacies and lewd play.

Shobha had written letters about these offences to her husband, an officer in the British Indian Armed Forces. He had been called away to deal with matters that were deemed of greater importance by the British, who were enacting their own rendering of god, scattering someone else's land, squandering someone else's blood. But the postal system, as decimated as everything else surrounding Shobha, misplaced her pleas for his help, his guidance, his instruction.

'I won't be able to do anything if they decide to come back for you,' Shobha said to the girl. 'Let me take you next door to the Khans. You'll be protected there.'

'No.' The servant girl was desperate. 'You don't understand. They were once our friends, our neighbours, our brothers. But none of them can be trusted now.'

'You can't return to your own family after what's been done to you,' Shobha explained to her, as gently as she could. 'And I can't keep you here. They'll come for you and hurt Keya, my own daughter, too. There are shelters for women like you in Amritsar and Delhi. We need to hide you until I can arrange for you to go there.'

'Let me die,' the young woman whispered. 'Please, all I ask is that the proper ceremonies are performed, the proper rites observed.'

Shobha took the girl into her arms, letting her own clothes, her own body, become soiled. The girl's blood dripped onto the floor, marking its territory, shaping the fate of everyone else in the house.

'Mama, what's wrong?' Shanti shook Mira. A frown marred her soft face as she climbed onto Mira's back and over her head, anxiously peering into her mother's face. Mira found that she was on all fours, on the ground. Fragments of cups and saucers, like her own disjointed feats of memory, remained all around her. Shanti slid off her mother, teetering off balance as she reached the floor. Her knee grazed against a ceramic splinter and started to bleed. Mira picked her up. She lowered her mouth to Shanti's knee, sucking the wound as she held Shanti in her arms. Mira watched her transparent spit mingle with her daughter's dense blood. What the mind tries to forget, the body always remembers.

If there could be a virtuous outcome of the misfortunes that had befallen the Sharma household, it was the fact that Samuel joined their home. Mira walked into the kitchen one morning to find him standing by the stove, holding his hands over one of the gas burners he had lighted to warm himself. He looked as if he had walked out of a Dickensian workhouse or, more appropriately, a Somali refugee camp. He was beyond thin; skeletal, in fact. His clothes were threadbare and he shivered without suspension. Samuel drank heavily and had spent years drifting from job to job in a substantially inebriated state, and had been fired from each in rapid succession. Mira took him in without question. She needed a man around the house, mainly for security and for odd jobs that Wairimu couldn't manage. Samuel maintained the garden, or what was left of it, and drove Shanti to and from school every day. Samuel agreed to complete these tasks for a roof over his head and meals to eat. Mira promised to give him a salary when she had money. There was an unstated acknowledgement between Mira and Samuel that this was how things were meant to be.

In just weeks, Samuel gained weight, recovered some humanness about him. Mira then gave him an ultimatum.

'I don't care what you do on your own time,' she told Samuel in the kitchen one morning when he arrived to take his tea. 'But if you even once drink on the job when you are supposed to be looking after Shanti, you need to leave my home.'

'Ndiyo, mama, I will give it my best,' Samuel nodded solemnly, 'if it is to be that you stop the smoking of the cigarette.'

Mira gave him a withering look as he chortled into his tea, and repaired to her bedroom, seeking comfort in her dark solitude as she gave over the upkeep of her household and child to Wairimu and Samuel.

With no regard for the genial weather outside, Mira drew the curtains and covered herself with blankets. She turned on her side and pulled her knees to her chest. Without a preordained frame placed for her in which she could comfortably reside, Mira found herself unable, or unwilling, to cast her own character, to determine her own fate. Instead of attempting to rise against the afflictions that had retired into her existence, she allowed her helplessness to annotate a new rendition of herself. The swelling curtains let the sun filter through in needles of light. In the afternoon, things shifted and settled to the floor. The soft mounds of dust gleamed in the sun's rays and threw shadows on the wall. Mira saw an incarnation of herself, its image disfigured and obscured. Perhaps, if Mira had been awarded a keener view, one that encompassed more than the tableau of her own vulnerability, she might have been able to steer clear of that vestigial undertow, concealed beneath the surface, pulling her deep inside her darkness.

Mira saw this version of herself speaking with the neighbours. They called her Shobha. She didn't call them anything, but thought of them as a pair and addressed them by their last name in her head. The Khans had sat on the verandah, refusing to come inside, to take tea even. The Mission, they explained, is accepting every Hindu. The purpose, they stated, is to convert them to Christianity. Given the circumstances, it is too much of an affront, they declared, for you to become a Muslim. As a Christian, they said, you will be welcome in Pakistan. If you remain a Hindu, history will repeat itself, in more horrifying, bloody ways than you could ever imagine. They spoke with the confidence of prophecy, with the impudence of the majority. If you take a Bible in your hands, you will be left alone, your daughter will be saved. Shobha told them she would wait for her husband. He had, after all this time, sent word to prepare, to get ready to leave. She unwrapped her aanchal and poured jewels and gold, that glistened immodestly, from the end of her sari into their laps. My dowry, she whispered, take it, to look after Keya should anything happen to me. The shafts of undiluted aching in her eyes caused them to lower their own. And when they were finally able to meet her gaze, their faces were masked in darkness.

As Shanti watched her childhood, as she had known it, fall apart, Mira spent most of her time in bed, claiming that she was plagued with migraines. She kept the curtains drawn all day and never let the verandah door remain open, withdrawing into the cocoon she had fashioned for herself as protection against the exterior world. She inhabited this permanently eclipsed existence in her bedroom, shrinking into herself, becoming as much of a shadow as those that filled her room.

6

MIRA SAT OUTSIDE THE headmistress's office, waiting for the nun to receive her. She looked out of the window, watching the schoolchildren participate in their class activities. Below the window, young girls tilled the soil in rectangular patches, preparing to plant vegetables for their agriculture class. Beyond these shambas, an older group was building a mud hut, fashioning cakes of clay and manure with their hands, laying them on a structure of cement, sculpting dank walls that would retain moisture and keep the interior of the hut cool under the sun even at its most febrile position, at noon. Younger girls played on top of the hill under a few scattered thorn trees. They collected hay, arranging it in even lines to create organized camps. Mira thought she saw Shanti under a tree, a pale sylph-like spot among a sturdier, darker maze. She knew for certain that it was her daughter when the small figure sat cross-legged on the mud in one of the smaller areas divided by lines of hay, and let the other girls run their fingers through her hair, ruffling, pulling, braiding and knotting, as they felt a texture so different from what emerged from their own skin.

When they ran out of the money Mira had given them, Wairimu had persuaded Mira to get out of bed. Shanti's school fees had been overdue for more than six weeks, and Wairimu had received a phone call from Shanti's school, informing Mira that Shanti would no longer be welcome on school property unless the fees were paid by the end of the week. Mira, still struggling to surface from the well of her solitude, had been driven to Shanti's school by Samuel.

Forty-five minutes passed before the headmistress opened the door to her office and ushered Mira inside. The headmistress was not receptive to Mira's pleas to keep Shanti at the Loreto Convent school.

'Look, I'm sorry to hear of your financial troubles, but this president's been very good to us and I'm sure he has his reasons for terminating your finances. There's nothing we can do to help,' the headmistress told Mira as she flipped through a manila folder that had Shanti's name written on the cover with a black marker. 'Doesn't your own community have schools?'

'Yes, Sister, I assume they do, but I don't really belong to that community. I wasn't born here,' Mira replied in explanation. 'I was brought up in a convent in India, so even when my husband wanted to and we could afford it—' Mira faltered.

The headmistress raised her eyebrows and waited for her to continue.

'I never let Shanti be sent to study in England like my husband wanted. You see, it's important to me that my daughter be a Loreto girl as well.'

'A Loreto girl? Well, well,' said the nun. She examined Mira over the top of her reading glasses, taking in the picture of the woman standing in front of her, put together as roughly as a patchwork of discarded material. Fabrics that appeared as if they had once gleamed with promise but were cut out and left over from a grand design and were now too soiled for anyone to use. She looked at Mira's silk sari, the frayed edges warping the fall of the expensive cloth, strands of hair tumbling from the bun piled upon her head in perpetual motion, like leaves falling from a tree in autumn.

The headmistress patted down the blue habit covering her head and lightly dusted the matching blouse and skirt she was wearing. As though she were making sure that the peculiarity of the image before her hadn't travelled and contaminated her own pristine attire. She sat behind her desk and carefully looked through Shanti's file once more. Then she closed the folder and drummed her fingers on the cover.

She said to Mira, as a final statement rather than a question, 'And what, may I ask, is your religion?'

It was almost time for Shanti to go home when Mira returned to the car. She waited with Samuel in the parking lot for her daughter. Shanti walked out of the low school building, the white blouse and navy pleated skirt of her uniform streaked from sitting in the mud, her hair greasy from all the handling. She was surprised to find that her mother had left her curtained bedroom and was sitting, meticulously upright, in the passenger seat of their car, waiting for her.

'Shanti,' Mira said to her as soon as she climbed into the car. 'How do you feel about becoming a Christian?'

And so Mira was able to keep Shanti in the missionary school by agreeing to let her convert to Catholicism in lieu of school fees. The Loreto nuns embraced Shanti as a saved child and rushed to organize a late baptism and first communion for her, loaning her clothes for each event, so she could catch up with her classmates in their preparations for their confirmation ceremony. Mira did not attend any of these rituals, claiming that she was too ill to get out of bed.

Shanti was delighted with the result of the contrived mutation of her theological persuasion. She could finally join her schoolmates in taking communion during the weekly mass that was held in the school chapel every Wednesday morning. She no longer had to be excused from religion classes. The nuns would give her the biggest piece of fried fish when they served the students lunch in the cafeteria every Friday. The other girls accepted her as one of their own, allowing her to take on a fuller role in their camps of hay built around the velvety lime trunks of the thorn trees. She no longer had to be the doll sitting by herself in the smallest room until someone decided to settle down and braid her hair. Shanti elected to be the Mama of the camp one day, pretending to cook and clean for her brood, a herdsman the next, rounding up and directing the others so they could remain safe from any hungry lionesses on the prowl.

Shanti's knees were hurting from kneeling on the low wooden stool behind the pew. She clasped her hands together in a tight fist as she prayed with the fervor of the recently converted, waiting her turn in the confessional booth.

'Bless me, Father, for I have sinned,' Shanti recited in the exact manner she had been taught and as she had practised one hundred times before letting herself go to sleep the night before her first confession.

She could hear her heart knocking against her chest as she sat by herself in the corner of the chapel curtained off from the rest of the room. There was a small, square latticed window cut into the wall facing her. Curtains covered the other side of the window so Shanti couldn't see through it. She tried to remember what she was supposed to do next. Shanti humbly bowed her head to receive the Sign of the Cross, deciding that was the safest thing to do.

'I confess to Almighty God, to Blessed Mary ever Virgin, to all the Saints and to you, my spiritual Father, that I have sinned,' she whispered on the third try, her excitement only slightly deflated after two false starts.

'How long has it been since your last confession?' Shanti heard a disembodied voice from behind the curtains.

'This is my first confession,' Shanti said, heavy with the acknowledgement that she was guiltier than anyone else who had ever been in the school chapel. 'I was a Hindu before today.'

'And my mother, she's sick,' she continued, not giving the voice through the window a chance to respond. 'I think it's because she is a sinner.'

'What, my child, has she done to be seen as a sinner in the eyes of the Lord?'

The voice surprised Shanti. It was quiet and serious, so unlike the booming echo she'd been anticipating for almost a month. Shanti decided she needed to impress upon the voice the gravity of her particular situation. 'She refuses to convert. She refuses to come to any of my ceremonies. She stays in bed all day. Sister Headmistress told me in front of the whole class that she is acting sinfully.'

'Sister Petra should know that there is little one can do in the face of the sins of others except pray every day for their salvation.'

'I do, I pray every night.' Shanti covered her face with her hands and started to cry. 'I don't want her to go to hell. You see, she's a Hindu and Sister Headmistress said there weren't any cows in heaven, or anything else Hindus hold sacred.'

'The ideas of heaven and hell are something you and I can continue to talk about. And purgatory, too. There might, in fact, be a special place in purgatory for Sister Petra.'

The voice told Shanti to say ten Hail Marys every night. She left the curtained area with more questions instead of the answers she'd been expecting.

Shanti slowly turned the handle of the bedroom door. The rusty metal of the hasp protested its retreat. She cringed each time she heard its whiny creak, limning her mother's reaction beyond the door. Shanti removed her shoes before she entered the room and carefully tiptoed across the carpeted floor in an effort to muffle the impact of her advance.

Mira, who lay motionless in bed, under the ballast of a bedcover, two razais and a covering sheet in spite of the equable temperature of the day outside, heard her daughter's laborious progression into her bedroom. Shanti's efforts to mute the disruption caused by her entry only resulted in eliciting a greater wave of agitation from Mira. Poor, beloved Shanti, who was trying so hard not to disturb her. But there was nothing Mira could do for her. Her own melancholy prevented her from doing anything. It stopped Mira from giving Shanti what a daughter deserved. As if sensing this, Shanti only ever approached Mira as a last resort, which only made their entire interaction—Shanti's requests and Mira's inability to provide—all the more debilitating. Mira opened her eyes wide, forcing herself to focus and shutter the palpitating creature lying within the recesses of her head. It was like a coiled serpent, shifting lazily against her skull, pausing for moments, as if it had not yet made a decision to strike.

'Ma?' Shanti whispered tentatively when she finally reached the bed.

'Yes,' replied Mira. She sent strands of her afflicted disconsolation towards Shanti, not knowing how to protect the child from her failure.

'It's my birthday next week,' Shanti continued uncertainly.

'Of course it is,' Mira responded feebly, and a mist of guilt settled, creating dents in the crust of infirmity into which she had earlier, comfortably, withdrawn. Feeling the oiled predator within her shift, she lay back against her pillows and waited as it contemplated an incursion.

'Ma?' asked Shanti, biting the insides of her cheeks as if the air was being sucked out of her. 'Can I have a birthday party?'

Mira gave Shanti the best answer she could, and agreed.

At Wairimu's instruction, Shanti placed a wooden cup carved out of rosewood filled with cool water at Mira's bedside. The musky scent of the moist wood spread heavily through the room. Mira reached for the solid tumbler and sipped the aromatic liquid apprehensively, hoping it would not provoke the creature but instead have the desired effect of calming it. The woody bouquet travelled through her sinuses, curling into every cranny and crevice, quelling the onset of a headache for the moment. She turned towards the window and opened her eyes to the radiant brightness of the room.

Mira knew they could not have people over, with her house in its state of lapsed maintenance. She invited Lata to tea so she could ask if her friend wouldn't mind hosting the birthday party at their pool house. Mira assured Lata that the children would be no trouble. They would go nowhere near the main house. She would bring all the food and make sure to clean up afterwards. All Lata needed to do was to allow a group of children to use her pool for a few hours on a Saturday afternoon. Lata agreed, saying what she always did when the subject of children was raised, that although she and her husband chose not to have children of their own to avoid managing the clutter that children inevitably produce, they would be delighted to have some over on their grounds, for a limited time.

'And really, Mira, let me buy Shanti a party dress. I only ever see that child wearing her school uniform or P.E. kit.' Lata sighed as she gestured towards Shanti, who stood by her mother's bed. 'I know times are difficult for you; even I've been warned not to be seen spending time with you. Who knows what can happen. And Mohanji has such a prominent position in the country. Our president depends on his loyalty. But what kind of a Hindu would I be if I turned away from a friend in need? Of course we can celebrate Shanti's birthday at my house.'

Mira bit her lower lip and clasped Lata's hands in her own, thanking her.

'But you really must get out of bed and straighten yourself up, Mira,' Lata continued. 'People see you and talk. They say how dirty you and Shanti look, how your house is in such a shambles. You can't lie in this bedroom all day. And it's filthy.' Lata twitched her nose as she looked around Mira's dark, dank room.

'I like ma's room like this,' Shanti interrupted. 'It's good to play hide-and-seek in.'

'You're too little to know what state your mother's in,' Lata said. 'And little ears should not be flapping where they are not invited. Your mother shouldn't even let you see her in this condition. Where is your sense of shame, Mira?' Lata went back to reprimanding her friend as she shooed Shanti away.

7

ON SHANTI'S TENTH BIRTHDAY, Wairimu baked a cake and made jugs full of watered down orange-flavoured juice from the last, precious bottle of Lucozade that she had stored away for the occasion. Samuel brought some banana chips from the market. Mira managed to get out of bed, bathe and put on a summer dress. She dressed Shanti in the frock that Lata had given her for the party. It was too large and the material uncomfortably stiff. The frills on the sleeves poked into Shanti's skin. Mira turned the outfit into a grand joke until Shanti finally agreed to wear it. They pretended they were secretly having a costume party as part of Shanti's birthday celebrations and that she would win first prize if she put on Lata's gift, earning the title of 'Most Horrendously Dressed'.

Samuel drove Mira, Shanti and Wairimu to Lata's house. Three men stood on guard at the large, closed gates. They refused to let the car through. They said that Samuel was permitted to park outside, and Mira and Shanti could enter while the maid and the driver had to wait with the car. Mira refused, insisting that Wairimu and Samuel come in with them.

'My servants go wherever I go,' she said. 'Anyway, they have to help unload and set up for the party.'

The guards reluctantly let them in, phoning ahead to warn Lata of the people entering her property.

Samuel drove into the Patels' parking lot and parked their small Toyota next to three Mercedes Benzes. Shanti, Wairimu and Samuel stared in awe at the big house before them and the three sleek cars by their side. Mira was the only one of the four who had been there before, to attend dinner parties with Prashant and take coffee on Tuesday mornings with Lata and the other well-to-do Indian wives, when she was considered to be in the same league as them. But she gawked as well, since she hadn't been invited over since Prashant died.

Lata came out of the house, wringing her hands, her face contorted in wrinkles of worry, permanently ruining her beauty. She wore a patterned housecoat over her well-endowed figure which, Shanti thought, made her look like a brightly-coloured pin cushion, and competition for the first prize she thought she had secured with her own outfit.

'Really, Mira,' Lata said, by way of greeting, 'you could have warned me you were planning to bring your kaalas inside the gates. I had to quickly make sure the safe was locked but you haven't given me enough time to put away all the valuables.'

Shanti felt Samuel's and Wairimu's bodies tighten as she stood between them. In spite of the language barrier, Wairimu and Samuel recognized that they were being referred to in a derogatory manner. They both took a step back, towards the Sharmas' parked car.

'Don't be silly, Lata, there's nothing to worry about,' Mira said gaily from behind the shield of her large sunglasses, as she pushed Shanti in front of her. 'See how lovely Shanti looks in the dress you gave her.'

Lata stuck out a fat, pedicured foot encased in a pink lacy slipper from underneath her housecoat. 'My woman did quite a good job with the material I had left over from my bedroom slippers. Those shops in Switzerland are so finicky, they make you buy yards of unnecessary material. I usually throw out the cloth I don't need. But for once the poor darling looks halfway like a little girl should.'

'Yes, I was just telling Shanti that earlier,' Mira replied.

As Lata led them towards the pool area, the Sharma contingent followed glumly, the prospect of a celebration suddenly tedious. They found the pool house locked.

'I hope Shanti's friends come wearing their swimsuits. I can't have any of my buildings open, especially with your servants here,' Lata announced as three adults and one child turned expectantly towards her.

'We'll make do,' Mira said, a little too quickly for the others' comfort. 'And thank you again for your generosity. We'll be sure to call you and Mohan down when we cut the cake.'

'We have cake from the French patisserie that has opened nearby,' Lata said. 'Besides, your woman is a housekeeper, not a cook.'

Mira shot a desperate look at Wairimu, who kept her back to the two women as she started to set out the food on a stone ledge by the pool.

During the first half hour of the party, nine girls arrived, wearing frilly dresses, with swimming costumes and caps rolled up in towels and tucked under their arms. Samuel returned to the parking lot while the girls changed in the open air, giggling as they tried to catch each other in various states of undress.

Shanti felt a resurgence of joy as she splashed around the pool with her school friends; they were planning a swimming ballet to perform for Mira and Wairimu later in the day. Mira sat by the pool in the shade, wearing dark glasses and a large hat. She smiled feebly at Shanti, toiling to endure the rest of the afternoon outdoors and in the company of a group of children angling for her attention.

The party was interrupted when Lata, still wearing her housecoat in spite of the warm weather, charged down to the pool area. Her watchmen followed closely, wielding their batons in their hands.

She pitched herself in Mira's direction. The mass of her body weight propelled her forward faster than she could move her feet. She tripped over her pink lace bedroom slippers. The girls, watching from the pool, began to laugh and clap, delighted with the unexpected entertainment.

Mira sat upright, preparing herself to face Lata.

'How could you do this to me, Mira?' Lata said, leaning over Mira's puny frame as she tried to prevent the spectators from listening.

When Mira looked into Lata's eyes and saw the manic self-righteousness reflected in them, any shaving of hope she had of keeping her friend content until the party was over disintegrated.

'What is it now?' Mira asked, keeping her voice low as she stood up and tried to move them further away from the pool.

'You did this on purpose!' Lata said, unable to keep her voice to a whisper. She gestured at the pool with a jut of her chin. 'You wanted to drag me down too, by bringing these kaalis here.'

'They're Shanti's friends from school.'

The girls had stopped playing in the pool when they saw Lata and the guards rushing towards them. Shanti had quickly swum to the edge, close to where her mother and Lata stood, so she heard everything. She felt her skin prickle and the hair on her neck and shoulders stand on end. Her friends gathered in a small tight circle at the other end of the pool, next to the steps that would lead them out of the shallow water. Shanti knew she had suddenly been spun out of favour as they formed a barrier she knew she would not be able to break. They silently trooped out of the pool and put their clothes on over their wet bathing suits as if a collective decision to leave had been made.

Shanti saw her mother kneel on the ground before Lata and whisper something before pressing her palms together and drawing them to her chin. Shanti clambered out of the pool and ran to her mother.

'Get up. Have you lost your mind? Degrading yourself in this way,' Lata said. 'You think I don't know about your tamasha with that man? Just because you have no shame or sense, don't think you can pull me down to your level!'

Mira collapsed into tears, crumpling into a heap on the ground. Shanti put her arms around her mother. Lata, perhaps not knowing what to do, returned to her house with her guards.

When the girls were ready, one of them, who had been assigned by the group to talk to Shanti, walked up to her.

'We're going,' she said.

Shanti's friends returned to their drivers and cars waiting in the parking lot. Wairimu and Samuel packed up the untouched cake, juice and chips. They helped Mira, who could not stop crying, into the car.

As they drove home in silence, Shanti saw every particle that had assembled to provide her joy—the celebration of her birthday, her acceptance in school propelled by her recent Christianity, the possibility that her mother might re-emerge from the shadows of her dark solitude into a normal, happy, reliable person—dissolve forever.

8

WEEKS PASSED OVER SHANTI'S tenth birthday. Mira withdrew from the pretence of social interaction, into the welcoming darkness of her bedroom. Shanti decided not to go back to school and no one insisted otherwise. She spent her days hanging around Wairimu, as the housekeeper tried to make do, conjuring soup out of the vegetables she attempted to grow in their garden and with anything Samuel managed to get from the market with the little money Mira handed over. Wairimu set Shanti tasks around the house in order to pass the long, cheerless days, ordering her to shell peas so she could make a rice pulau one day, to dust the paltry pieces of furniture that were left in the house another day.

Shanti had nightmares every night. Wairimu decided to stay in the house to take care of her. She carried in the sisal mat from her room in the servants' quarter and laid it down on the floor in the hallway outside the bedroom where Shanti slept. She got up every twenty minutes to check on Shanti, stroking her gently, sponging off the sweat on her body, and cleaning any mess she had purged during her dreams. Mira tried to stay up with Shanti for a few nights but she wasn't able to manage. Shanti would be fine, Wairimu assured Mira, and made her go and sleep in her own room while Wairimu remained sleeping on the floor outside Shanti's door.

When the lights were out one night, Shanti went to Wairimu to ask her to sleep on the bed in the guestroom. But she refused.

'And what will your mother say when she is better and sees me? She will not like and I do not like,' she whispered fiercely. 'Go back to bed before I forget you are a big girl and beat you with my shoe.'

For the first time in her life, Shanti recognized that servants were so much a part of her household and yet not part of her family. People who had servants often forgot that their help had their own families, their own loyalties. And all the time they were watched by these servants, who formed their own understanding and cast their own perceptions of their employers' actions. Shanti and Mira were foreigners, visitors, for all purposes guests in someone else's country. Shanti knew that if she was able to glean their servants' inner thoughts about her family, the information about thc intimate occurrences in their lives, she would be ashamed. The comprehension of how much others knew about them and the judgement that she would then have to make on herself and her mother was too awful.

As each member of the Sharma household, in his or her own manner, succumbed to a languorous existence free of structural conventions, the days flitted by like elusive shadows in the strong beams of sunlight over the African plains.

One morning, Mira sat in the verandah outside her bedroom and surveyed the landscape. The air was quite still. Two palm trees in the garden swayed lazily in the light breeze, whispering as they bent over Shanti who was playing hopscotch below. There were a few weaverbirds darting through the flame trees. A hawk circled lazily above them in the bright blue sky. A long car, as lean as a leopard and just as swift, glided into the open gates and across the gravel path. Mira closed her eyes, enjoying the last minutes of calm in the day as she prepared for the schism in the mosaic of insulation into which she had retired.

Lata stepped out of the air-conditioned, leather-enswathed interior of her car and walked up to the Sharmas' house. She kept her pug-like nose tilted upwards, her large eyes which were accentuated with heavy doses of eye shadow were half closed, her plumped ruby-red lips were compressed as she avoided any sort of communication with Samuel, who had come to help her out of the car, and Wairimu, who opened the door to let her into the house. Lata made her way to Mira's bedroom, climbing the stairs without holding the railing for support. She walked through the master bedroom to the verandah where Mira sat, waiting in silence.

Lata had a proposal, a plan to alleviate any guilt that had been resting heavily on her, and a transaction, a weighing in of emotional commitment, to ward off any sense of obligation she may have been feeling towards her friend.

As ill-fortune and dire inconvenience would have it, Lata's sister in England had sent her son to stay with the Patels over the summer after his graduation from university. In addition to Lata's and Mohan's already well-honed inclination against children, dogs, cats, youths and other creatures of that same ilk, the young man who had imposed himself on the immense Patel estate seemed to have fallen in with a company of troublemakers. He had begun consorting with a peculiarly anarchistic community: a collection of sons and daughters of foreigners in Africa, all of whom had some connection to Kenya from their childhood. They had returned from the First World to live in Nairobi. Their reasons for coming back varied: they had encountered a failure of some sort in their experiences in efficient markets and societies; they had Africa in their blood, like malaria, a recurring disease they couldn't expunge from their being; they had succumbed to the allure of an easy, comfortable existence, hanging onto it for dear life because the awareness that it could be wrenched away from them at any moment lurked beneath the surface of all things; they had returned to drink away their personal demons. They lived a frenzied life with no rules or order amid the possibility of imminent violence.

Lata had felt a sudden, immediate desire to make the Sharmas the object of her generosity. The young man was to spend the summer with Mira and Shanti. In return, the Patels wanted to send Shanti to a school in England. The school had been informed of a scholarship student who would be joining them in the fall under the umbrella of the Patels' benevolence. This was no place to raise a young girl, especially given Mira's difficult circumstances, Lata pronounced. And Lata's nephew would tutor Shanti during the summer so she could catch up with the weeks of school she had missed.

The entire household sagged as Mira unquestioningly accepted Lata's offer. Mira held Lata's hand to her unbathed breast.

'Oh, Lata,' she said, her voice thick with tears. 'You don't know how cursed I am, all alone, all over again, with a daughter I don't know what to do about.'

Shanti, who had followed Lata into the house and had been lurking at the threshold of the verandah the whole time, retreated into the shadows of her mother's room. She braced herself for another intruder into their home.

9

THE SHARMA HOUSEHOLD BENT to Lata's will in the days that followed. The house and all the people in it were scrubbed clean. The pantry was filled with food. The sisal mat outside Shanti's bedroom door was rolled up and Wairimu was made to move back into her quarters and wear her uniform. Samuel was told not to enter the house unless he received an explicit request to do so.

Ash was then welcomed into the Sharmas' home. He had his instructions from Lata in hand. He was to help a girl, less fortunate than he, who would benefit from his family's benevolence and from his privileged foreign education and manners.

Ash had warm brown eyes fringed with curly eyelashes and soft, wavy black hair. He had dimples whenever he smiled (which was all the time). He sported a perpetual suntan with the help of the strong African sun. He was also constantly sloshed with a continuous supply of Tusker Baridis. No matter how hard Shanti tried, she could not hate him.

As it turned out, Ash quite liked his ten-year-old tutee, instructing her more in the skills she would need to survive boarding school in England than in any academic subject. However, he had trouble playing the responsible house guest in the sultry atmosphere of this city so close to the equator. Mira was the perfect paramour: old enough to offer him experience but still young enough to be attractive, unattached, unfettered by Nairobi society's conventional mores. He serenaded her in true African bwana style. It was spectacular—and precarious, as most things here were.

Mira blossomed like a flower that had been freed of the confines of a clay pot, setting her gloomy reflections aside as she flourished under his gaze. Mira realized that even though he was just twenty-four, Ash possessed an authority in this part of the world, as a well-to-do foreign-educated Indian male. He ushered Mira back into the social circles from which she had been thrown out, inviting her to the parties the Patels held in their home.

During one dinner party, fortified by several Tuskers, Ash proposed to Mira—or was it propositioned; she couldn't remember through her own gin-and-tonic haze—in the soft moonlight under the stars by the pool outside his aunt's house, as they stood near a row of tables covered with brightly dyed kangas with hors d'oeuvres laid out prettily on them. The buzzing of bottle-green flies and whiffs of the carcass of a goat roasting over a crackling spitfire close by heightened the electricity. The silhouettes of servants standing nearby, ready to serve if beckoned, magnified their awareness of each other. But the eyes keenly watching Mira and Ash also delineated the borders of their excess; their presence was a reminder that word would be sent, a story spun, if they were to fall too far, step too deep, into the temptations that surfaced in the night.

The next morning, during a celebratory brunch for no specific reason but that someone felt like celebrating the idea of a brunch, at a lodge near Ngong Hills, Ash demanded the jazz band play 'Summertime', a serenade to Mira, as a token of his regard. He ordered the silent servers in white gloves to ply her with Bloody Marys while they stared at the purple mountains under watery-blue skies. The melodies of Miles Davis wafted around them as their backs were turned to his aunt, his relatives, the other guests—they didn't hear the low whispers that spread through the crowd like an African brush fire.

One morning, Ash drove Mira out of the city to a country club in a small town called Naivasha—joined by friends in a caravan of cars, to serve as a deterrent to any potential carjackings that might occur along the way. Later that afternoon, champagne flutes in hand, the two of them wandered across the gardens, down to the pier and gazebos on the shore; they took boat rides across the lake, floating alongside families of hippos and clusters of crayfish; they waded through the water hyacinth, that deceptive weed which was so beautiful above the surface and strangled beneath. A dinner reception started in the early evening as flocks of seagulls flew across the open skies. Ash danced with Mira on the shores of Lake Naivasha deep into the velvety night, their bodies barely outlined by the open log fires. He replenished Mira's goblet of Irish coffee as he led her away from Nairobi society's arched stares. Askaris stood at the edges, keeping guard to ensure that no robbers attacked them from the surrounding shores. The chirping crickets wove a web of tales, a tapestry of Mira's susceptibility and Ash's seduction.

The real seduction lay in the impermanence of the moment. Their romance was heightened by a raw, natural abandon, a sense of personal insecurity pervasive in the air. They were captured in the clutches of the decadence that surged through the soil, the skies, the moon, the air; that emerged in flashes and ultimately left them holding nothing.

Shanti was Mira's helper, her shadow through it all. She picked out what she thought were the finest saris and most stunning jewellery out of the few things her mother still had left. She ironed the silk and wrapped Mira's body with it. She clasped intricate gold necklaces around Mira's neck and adorned her wrists with gold bangles. She helped Mira comb her hair, weaving sweet scents into it as she dipped the comb in rose water before running it across every strand. Shanti, afraid of sleep and the prospect of battling her nightmares on her own, stayed awake, waiting for Mira when she crawled in during the early hours of the morning, exhausted, her kohl smudged, her sari barely wrapped around her. Shanti made her mother tea and they sat at the dining table while Mira told her stories from the night before.

Or they curled up on the sofa with Ash between them, when he came home with Mira. Her mother talked without interruption, as if she'd learned again how to speak, and Shanti listened and watched her mother fawn over the young man.

Mira turned Shanti into her personal maid, her aide, her truest confidante. She never once considered that Shanti might have been flailing, as she stood on uneven ground as the third, least popular, most dispensable member of their newly-formed trio.

Shanti tucked away in the recesses of her most private thoughts the knowledge that her mother was only happy when there was another person, a man, to take her away from Shanti. No matter how hard she tried to bury this little fact, it prevailed, assuming its own misshapen, ugly form as it whispered confirmation of Shanti's solitary, neglected existence during the summer before her departure.

Meanwhile, the empty house filled with the lightness that Mira had let Ash weave around her. Blinded by her recently found happiness, Mira was oblivious to her daughter's own journey inward, the disapproval displayed by Wairimu and Samuel when they caught brief glimpses of the interactions, and the further denouncement by the Indian community in Nairobi.

10

ALL OF MIRA'S ADVERSITIES seemed to have evaporated during these brief months. David Silverstein, Prashant's attorney, made a visit to the house. He told her the inquiry about the lawyer associated with Prashant's business dealings had been lifted and that Prashant's assets were once again in Mira's possession. Over the next few weeks, the house was refurnished, servants were rehired, gifts were endowed and debts repaid. Mira asked Silverstein to set up a savings plan for Wairimu and Samuel so they could use their own resources if something like this happened again. The lawyer wanted her to review the papers to make sure it was what she wanted. Mira responded by asking Silverstein to make sure that what he had drawn up was what Wairimu and Samuel wanted.

Silverstein and Mira sat at the dining table, the papers detailing the pension plans for the servants spread out before them.

Samuel entered the dining room with his cap in his hands. Mira asked him to join them at the table but he demurred, shaking his head meekly as he continued to stand by himself, shifting the cap back and forth between his hands.

Silverstein elaborated on the pension he had drafted for the driver. The lawyer spoke very slowly, Mira thought, enunciating each word a little too carefully. Mira tried to hurry him along, indicating that she knew Samuel too well to do this to him, she knew his ability to grasp matters. But Silverstein brushed her aside. He wanted to make sure Samuel understood what he was saying as he described the details of the income that was to be given to him from the Sharmas' savings on a monthly basis.

Mira slouched in her chair, feeling entirely meek as well. This man, she realized, was inextricably woven into the fabric of her daughter's childhood. He was one of a mere handful of people she considered to be part of Shanti's small family. He was the same age as Prashant.

When Silverstein was finally satisfied that Samuel understood the terms of his retirement, he called him to the table to sign the papers. Samuel stood before them, pen in one hand, cap in the other. He did not know how to write. Silverstein was unperturbed and smoothly pulled out an inkpad from his briefcase. He showed the driver how to press his left thumb into the moist pad and press it onto the papers in lieu of a written signature.

The paperwork finally completed, Samuel turned to Mira. He bowed in her direction, his arms outstretched, his palms clasped together. Mira took his hands in her own and Samuel quickly adjusted his fingers to ensure that Mira's hands were not sullied by the ink smudges on his fingers.

'Is this all right?' Mira asked Samuel uncertainly. 'Because if you're not happy with anything, we can always change it.'

Samuel shook his head. 'You have been good to me, not only talking-talking, like some other bwanas.'

Mira was very tired by the time Wairimu came into the dining room. The housekeeper smoothed her hands on her apron as she stood on the same spot as Samuel had.

When she hesitated after Mira asked her to sit down, Mira said impatiently, 'For heaven's sake, Wairimu, sit down as you always do when it is just you and me.'

Wairimu joined them at the dining table, pouring herself a cup of the tea she had prepared and helping herself to a slice of cake that she had earlier baked.

Silverstein gave Wairimu the option of receiving her pension as a lump sum or in an annuity stream of payments.

She sat upright and answered him proudly, even a little scornfully, 'When I first started working for this family, Shanti's father, Bwana Sharma, helped me open a savings account. I will use that money to run my own duka in town, and this retirement money to buy the property for my house in my village. I don't want to live on someone else's land.'

'But you will remain in my employment for now, won't you?' Mira asked her.

'As long as Shanti is here. Now that we have our money, we can send Shanti to a proper school here. We do not need that woman, yes?'

'Yes, I suppose,' Mira said uncertainly.

'It is settled then,' said Wairimu, wiping the cake crumbs off her uniform and placing them on the table in front of Mira and her lawyer.

Shanti grinned idiotically at Wairimu as the housekeeper related her conversation with the dexterity and panache Shanti knew all too well. Shanti could not remember the last time her heart felt so light.

'Aiee, Shanti, if you keep smiling like that, you will burst open,' Wairimu scolded Shanti.

Shanti hugged Wairimu. 'And I will stay with you, my girl,' Wairimu said into Shanti's ear. 'I cannot leave while you are still here.'

11

LIFE SEEMED TO RESUME normalcy in Nairobi. The attempted coup and the subsequent rash of violence were forgotten, or at least hidden away. The president and those who were in his favour entrenched their power, skimming each tranche of money the country received, taking a cut of every deal that was made and a portion of all transactions delivered. The foreign press, heavily regulated inside the country, took to referring to the nation's leader as *C'est Moi—It is Moi, It is Me, It is all Me, It is all Mine*—as he grew to be one of the wealthiest men in the world. It was only much later that the ruin conferred onto the country could no longer be ignored. When multilateral institutions pulled out, development was stunted and the quality of life declined for more of the population. It was only then, as poverty burgeoned across the land and insecurity settled like a permanent fog across the capital, that foreigners were advised to move first into communal inhabitations and then out of the country for good.

The three months ended and, amidst rumours and condemnation, Ash prepared to leave for England. During his last week in Nairobi, he didn't come to the Sharmas' house, he didn't return Mira's phone calls. The night before Ash was to leave, Mira stayed awake, hoping he would phone her.

Mira thought about where it had begun and when she should have stopped it, withdrawn before she felt too much, fell in too deep. When she first laid eyes on Ash the morning he arrived at their home, she should have had the strength to look away. During Ash's first tutoring session with Shanti, Mira had left her bed and walked through the rooms of her house, looking for a book, when she saw Ash sitting with Shanti in the dining room. He had looked up from the papers on the table and smiled. Ash's eyes, a crystalline brown, exuded self-assurance. Mira recognized his easy charming smile, his ability to extend his hand, lend his heritage, that brand of approval, to her insubstantial family.

Ash had stood up from the dining table and invited Mira to join the lesson. He told her he liked beautiful things and gestured to the African carvings hanging on the walls as his eyes lingered on her neck, caressing the burnished skin that lay bare. Mira wondered if she really was beautiful to him. She was so unlike the young girls he must know in England, with their learned accents and posh manners, their translucent skins and easy smiles.

The telephone woke Mira. She had fallen asleep in front of the television, the shining images and distorted sounds adding to her disturbed dreams.

'I've woken you.'

'No, no. I mean you have, but it doesn't matter,' Mira mumbled into the phone, scrambling to surface into consciousness.

'I'm sorry about not being in touch. It's just that—' Ash stopped short and gave an embarrassed laugh. 'Well, I've time to talk now if you want to.'

'I'm not going to send Shanti to school in England. We will live without the fetters of your aunt's charity.'

'I've decided to stay on, too. I've found a job here with Oxfam. And an apartment, so I won't be living with Lata and Mohan.'

'When were you going to tell me?' Mira asked. 'I have to see you again,' she said, after receiving no answer.

'I don't know.'

'Please, Ash.' Mira's voice was frantic. 'Please let me see you tonight.'

On their last night together, Mira knew this was the end. She was at the door, waiting for him. She was ready. They did not wait to take their clothes off but made love desperately, clawingly, like animals, in the hallway. Mira became limp while Ash drank in all of her, bathing and soaking and drowning as she tried to keep a part of him. She let him mark her. He bit and pierced and grazed her flesh. When Ash pulled away there was blood on her abdomen and on his. They traced their fingertips through their drying, mingled blood.

'Joined in blood,' Mira said. 'Now I have imprinted you inside me and me inside you.'

Would he always find this evening inside him, Mira wondered, or would he no more be able to seek it out than a single star from the multitude that sit in the sky?

The next morning Wairimu opened the door to the verandah in Mira's bedroom.

'That boy is a harlot!' Wairimu declared. 'He spends the night with you but he makes no promises.'

'But Wairimu, I thought you said that women like you and me don't need to be married.'

'That is different. We are different, you and me. We do not need to marry men who we have to feed while they drink our money away. No, we just need babies, like our Shanti. But that harlot, he will live with you under the same roof, unwed.'

For Wairimu there was a world of difference. She had birthed many children, not all from the same man, but she had not married even once. She refused to be traded like cattle and have her wages beholden to any man; she would not renounce her independence. However, the idea that a man and a woman could actively live together with no evidence of marital bonds was a severe assault on her Christian sensibilities.

'Anyway, he's gone,' Mira told Wairimu. 'And you're right,' she added, letting her fingers stroke the fresh marks on her abdomen and inner thighs. The bruises shivered under her touch, like the skin of a ripe fruit, ready to burst open. 'I'm finished with men. We have to survive on our own now.'

'It is the right thing,' Wairimu agreed.

12

AS THE DAYS OF that whimsical year blended into each other, the Sharmas' life, pressed and gummed together, seemed constructed to fall apart, no more permanent than a dream.

It happened in the first week of September. The women—Shanti considered herself one of them, she felt quite grown-up now that she was almost eleven and held an important position in the household as the binder of their trio, the thing that caused Wairimu to remain with them—had gone to their rooms to sleep. The doorbell rang. By the time Mira came downstairs, Wairimu was already standing at the open door, holding the side of her face where she had just been hit.

'Good evening, Mrs Sharma,' said Francis Gichuku, rubbing his left palm over his closed right fist. 'It is time. My guards have your man. I will give you an hour to pack your things.'

Mira tried to look past the minister to see what his men were doing to Samuel.

'Don't waste your time on trivialities, Mrs Sharma. You have one hour to get your daughter and take what you can.' His voice was flat, his impatience quietly ticked under the surface as he emphasized each syllable, like a bomb waiting to explode. It had a calming effect on Mira as she turned away from Wairimu and moved automatically up the stairs to Shanti, already making a mental list of the things she could manage to pack into the car.

Mira woke Shanti and told her to get dressed. She gave her a suitcase and said she could take what she was able to fit into it. Then she went back downstairs, walking past the minister without looking at him. She told Wairimu to fill the kikapus in the closet with whatever Wairimu could pack from the kitchen, dining room and living room within an hour. Then Mira went back upstairs and changed out of her nightgown into a salwar kameez and comfortable walking shoes. Shanti asked Mira where they were going. Mira didn't respond as she filled a suitcase with her jewellery, the money she had kept under her petticoats in her cupboard, her mother's recipes, a portrait of Prashant, family photographs and any clothes that could be packed into the spaces in-between.

The minister didn't offer to help as the three women carried the suitcases and baskets to the car. His policemen leaned against the land rover they had arrived in as they smoked cigarettes and watched the women load the car. The handles of their rifles were wedged in the gravel by their feet, the butts rested casually against their hips. Samuel was sitting in the driver's seat and none of the women dared call out to him.

Once everything was loaded, Wairimu sat in the backseat, the kikapus next to her. Mira made Shanti climb into the front passenger seat with her. Shanti didn't protest. Samuel rested both hands limply on the steering wheel while he stared straight ahead. His hands had been pounded with the policemen's rifles, stamped on with their boots and then dragged against the sharp stones that lined the gravel driveway. Mira made Shanti sit on the handbrake, the gear box between her legs. She leaned across her daughter to start the car and told Shanti to put it in gear. Samuel manoeuvered the steering wheel with his wrists and pushed the accelerator with his bare feet. The policemen hadn't let him put on his shoes when they hauled him out of his bed in the servants' quarter, dragging his body, clad only in a pair of khaki shorts, on the ground behind them. Slowly, bumpily, the car made its way down the driveway.

Outside the gate, Shanti asked Mira if she should help Samuel turn the steering wheel left or right. Mira said it didn't matter which direction they went. She started to tear her cotton dupatta into long strips and handed them to Wairimu. Wairimu poured hot water from a flask into a bowl, both of which she'd taken out of the kikapu. She sprinkled salt into the water from the salt shaker she'd retrieved from the cabinet only minutes before. She soaked each strip of cotton and handed it back to Mira, who applied the wet cloth on Samuel's hands. Samuel screamed in pain as the bandage was wrapped around his hands to hold together his torn flesh and fractured bones.

They drove away from their home in silence. It was the time that was neither night nor day. Steam was rising from the streets and unfurling in the air. There were shadows in the mist, floating by in an eerie quiet. Surrounded by the sleeping indifference of privilege, the workers of the city had stirred and were making their way to their functions in poverty, silence, acquiescence. Their car drove past askaris in uniform either travelling to or from their guard shift, mechanics and engineers on bicycles, cooks and servants waiting for matatus.

The highway was deserted when they got on it. Mira started to cry, her body started to shake.

'Keya,' whispered Mira. 'Keya, Keya, Keya.'

Mira turned back towards the night. She searched for it, for the memory that beckoned to her like a whisper beyond the swaying trees, calling out to her from the deep recesses of the sky. It whispered her name in the same longing tones she used, as though it were familiar with her grief, her fear. The African sky stretched over them, sheltering her from the secrets that lay beyond. She closed her eyes to escape into another time and place when she was made to pack a carload of her possessions. Mira let herself journey towards the heart of that mystery, that memory of a life that was and wasn't her own. Mira saw herself leave the car, Samuel's broken hands, Shanti sitting next to her, the drive away from her home, heading nowhere. She knew that once she arrived there, deep within its heart, she would find a piece of herself.

PART TWO

India

13

Long years ago we made a tryst with destiny, and now the time comes when we shall redeem our pledge, not wholly or in full measure, but very substantially. At the stroke of the midnight hour, when the world sleeps, India will awake to life and freedom. A moment comes, which comes but rarely in history, when we step out from the old to the new, when an age ends, and when the soul of a nation, long suppressed, finds utterance.

—Jawaharlal Nehru: Excerpt of Speech on the Granting of Indian Independence, August 14, 1947

SHOBHA TURNED THE DIAL of the rickety tuner until Prime Minister Nehru's voice was drowned out by the commotion of mass radio waves. It was August 15, 1947, and India had finally gained her independence. Shobha wiped away the tears that travelled down her face. It was an auspicious day. She should perform her puja, she told herself, thank Vishnu and Krishna—and Nehruji—for the blessings that brought freedom. She smoothed the wrinkles on her forehead, massaging the deep worry lines embedded in her skin. Her husband was right when he sent word to pack their belongings and prepare to leave their home. Independence had been granted to their homeland but they had found themselves on the wrong side of the line. They were in Pakistan.

Shobha's husband was posted in the northern region of Punjab. He had sent Shobha explicit instructions: she was to sort through their belongings; distribute things among neighbours to store for them until they could return or send for the items at a later date; and keep only the valuable things, things that could fit in the car he would arrive in to take her and their daughter across the border into India. He had also told her to procure two jerry cans of petrol. They would need these for the trip.

Shobha was unsure of what she had been told to do. How could she be expected to decide, all on her own, what had value and what hadn't? Some things were clearly valuable: her jewellery, the gold coins they had received as a wedding gift, the wad of rupees her husband kept stored in his cupboard. But what else could she add to that pile? Her wedding saris? The pieces of glass bangles—the bangles she had worn and he had smashed on their wedding night—that she had carefully stored all these years to commemorate the beginning of their shared life together? Would he deem those shards of broken glass valuable? And what about the fans? The summer had brought with it a drought this season, rendered bearable only by the operation of the fans. Surely it would be as dry and dusty where they were going? The monsoons were late this year and the heat that bore down into the long, windless days had made the fans extremely valuable items, essential for any household. Would her husband agree? To be on the safe side, Shobha decided to take just one of the fans with her.

And so the choices to carry or store aside were made. In areas where she was uncertain—which turned out to be many, as her husband hadn't told her where exactly they would be going or what conditions might exist there—she kept one of several general household items and set aside the rest to give away. Finally, she had a carload of valuables, which included one fan, one kitchen utensil, one set of sheets, a silk carpet, a handmade doll for her daughter, one frock out of the several frilly angrezi dresses her husband liked to see their daughter wear. The rest they would come back for, or rather, come back to, she hoped. In the meantime, those things would have to be relegated to memory.

A medley of conflicting emotions had splayed through Shobha these past months as she sorted and packed her life away. Fear had sliced through her stock of hope that life would remain as it always had, as stories of the terror that skirted the edges of her existence climbed over the walls and settled inside her home. Stories of unspeakable horrors and carnage clung to and dangled from the branches of the peepul tree in the courtyard outside. They shed the leaves of their sorrow outside her home at the slightest rustle or intimation of a breeze.

Violence—Hindus and Sikhs pitted against Muslims—spread across the north-west frontier as talks of a proposed division of India along religious lines were transmitted throughout the land. Both sides scarred, maimed and murdered. Shobha heard stories of men who rampaged through villages and towns, using religion as an excuse to brand symbols of their own beliefs on women's bodies.

By way of the whispering leaves of the Buddha's tree, Shobha heard the story of the train coming from India to Pakistan, filled with the bodies of Muslims who had been massacred by Hindus. The train had been packed with mutilated carcasses; in one compartment lay gunnysacks filled with women's breasts. She learned of Muslims pillaging through towns and forcing themselves on Hindu women who were found hiding in their homes and temples, before killing them or leaving them to die. Shobha heard of men in uniform—the police force and the army—of both religions serially raping women and selling them when they had turned to them for assistance.

Shobha heard stories of martyrdom and self-sacrifice for the sake of honour in the face of these terrors. Sikh women and children in one village had jumped into a well, choosing to drown themselves than be subject to the atrocities that lay in wait for them, and to escape the inevitability of being forced to convert to the religion of their torturers; one Hindu man beheaded his wife and four children at his wife's request while Muslim men rippled through his village, slowly but surely approaching his home; a Muslim man shot his family and then himself on a bus when it was halted on its journey and surrounded by a mob of Sikh men. Shobha heard of women seeking shelter in their place of worship—whether mosque, temple or gurdwara. They had poured kerosene around the edifice and set themselves on fire when the rioting men stormed towards them.

After hearing these stories, the origins of doubt took root within Shobha. It flourished and grew strong, the thick vines spread wide, fracturing the foundations of her belief. She started to question everything in which she had once placed her faith. Shobha wondered if her husband had been complicit in these crimes. If men who had lived side by side, as brethren, could turn on each other, what would stop her husband from doing the same? She lost her faith in god: she couldn't see where the existence of a merciful deity fit amid this carnage as stories of senseless violence poured into her home, the home to which she could no longer belong.

'Mama,' Keya sighed as she turned in her sleep.

Shobha went to the cot and smoothed her daughter's furrowed brow. As she stood over her child, watching her dream, she knew she must believe, for the sake of her daughter, that god existed. The alternative—a destiny not navigated by a supreme being—was too bleak to contemplate. She looked down at her daughter's sweet face and blew lightly on the closed eyes, on the curly lashes resting on those beloved plump cheeks, while Keya slept on, blissfully unaware of the dangers that gathered close by.

In the first light of dawn, Shobha lit two incense sticks and a diya. She covered her head, folded her palms and sat down to recite her prayers.

The monsoon arrived in a different form this year. It began as a seedling disturbance, an imbalance sparked by the friction of contending masses, igniting horror from each chafing glitch in the earth and sky. One wave after another spread across the land in a turbulent procession of fervor and recrimination. Communal peoples banded together; impending storms of violence began to circle. Then the conflicting winds began spinning. Low-lying villages were flooded and small homesteads were parted from their moorings. Walls started crumbling, pigs and cows started flying, mosques and temples started losing their roof tiles; whole villages were battered if not wrecked. Along the border, the battling winds began to pick up and gushed louder and stronger. Any person still standing was struck down and stripped of all that was recognizably human. One body after the next buckled, snapped and splintered in the face of the onslaught; heads and limbs were torn away and vanished into the spinning wind.

They hacked through the streets like a pack of rakshasas, demons driven by hate. Their long black hair, let loose, flew behind them; their beards, unrolled, streamed down their chests. With their nostrils flared and their fever-stricken eyes unnaturally wide, they screamed for blood. The Sikh men moved in a mass of dark cloud, brandishing kirpans, knives, swords, sickles above their heads. The curved blades of their sickles looked like a series of new moons glinting in the dark as they travelled towards their target, the very people who revered the sighting of a crescent shape in the sky. With a force that lay within them, beyond them, behind them, they were propelled forward. They struck down their weapons, beheading, mutilating, branding every Muslim they could find. They raped and killed until nothing was left unmarked by their hatred. As the hours stretched into the night, the new moon in the sky turned from silver to crimson.

Deep in her dreams, Keya wasn't sure what was happening but she knew that whatever it was, it was terrible. All she could hear was the angry howling of the wind. The sound was so loud; the gusts came at her with a deep, deep vibration that made her cringe. Keya realized with alarm that she could see it. It had become a solid, visible force around her. She could see the masses of storm physically hurtling towards her. It wasn't absolutely pitch black; she was in a wet, grey murk, with these twisting, shimmering bodies tearing through. The atmosphere was heavy with salt. Then Keya realized what the salty taste was: it was the taste of blood.

As Shobha waited for her husband to arrive in the army vehicle the next morning, she sensed that something was not right. There was no flicker of movement, not one sound that indicated life as she stood in the courtyard outside her house with her daughter, bundles of possessions and two jerry cans of petrol by her side. She didn't know what else she could do but wait. She had obeyed her husband's instructions to the last detail. The house was empty and locked. She was packed and ready for him to come and fetch her.

It was too late when Shobha heard them.

A raging beast unfurled in the dry dust of summer. Her skin tightened in fear as she heard a bloodcurdling cry: 'Pakistan!'

'Zindabad!' the beast howled in reply.

As they entered the gates, she could feel the ground tremble beneath her. The house shook behind her. Thc peepul tree in the courtyard was bent backwards and ripped out by its roots as the beast raged forward.

Shobha looked at her daughter's perplexed expression. As she stared into the child's large innocent eyes, eyes that implored her for an explanation, Shobha knew she had to believe.

'Keya, do as I say,' she said urgently, cupping her daughter's face in her hands. 'Run next door to the Khans. They are our neighbours, they will look after you.'

She hugged her daughter, feeling the tiny body against her for the last time. 'Go now, dearest. And promise me: don't look back.'

Keya turned and ran, wondering why her mother had decided to take a bath in the open like that, pouring liquid on herself from the jerry can. She ran and ran, behind the house, through the garden and over the wall. The sharp stones cut into her soft skin as she fell, but she felt no pain. Keya could sense nothing as she continued to run. Nothing, except the smell of her mother's burning flesh as Keya ran to meet her tryst with destiny.

PART THREE

Kenya

14

MIRA HAD COME TO the airport to receive Shanti. She looked small and lost in the crowd at Jomo Kenyatta International Airport. She was holding a walking stick and leaned her frail body upon it.

'Hi, ma,' Shanti said brightly as she walked up to her mother. Her greeting echoed falsely in the large hall, and she hung her head. 'You didn't have to come to pick me up.'

Shanti broke Mira's heart. After all these years, all these moments of worrying about her, she was only allowed the chance to set eyes upon her own daughter for a few hours at the most in any given week even though they inhabited the same house. Given permission by her own daughter, no less. There was what Mira could only call a sheepish expression on Shanti's face. The kind she used to get when she had failed to live up to her own expectations and then tried to pretend that none of it really mattered anyway. Shanti seemed aware that Mira could see this and seemed to be embarrassed by all of it, by the sight of Mira, even.

Mira let go of her walking stick and cupped Shanti's face in her hands, letting her bony fingers sink into her daughter's healthy skin. Shanti could not return her steady gaze and her eyes flickered around the airport lounge, aware of the strangers staring at them. After a moment, Shanti drew back, straightening her spine.

'Ma,' she offered in appeasement.

Mira let go of Shanti and leaned on her stick. Her eyes wandered over Shanti's body, taking in every part of her. Shanti felt shabby next to Mira's neatly clad figure in a pastel chiffon sari. She knew her mother thought that her t-shirt was too tight, that her jeans hung too low on her hips.

'Thank you,' Mira finally said.

'For what, ma?'

'For coming back.'

Shanti could not offer her a reply. She felt guilty, mired in the knowledge that she was only supposed to have been away for a fortnight. Mariella, her friend from school, and Shanti had forged a letter informing their families that the school trip that never existed in the first place had been extended by two weeks so the two girls could remain at the coast where they had rented a beach house on their own. Shanti could sense the edges of Mira's disappointment. So much, too much, had happened, and Shanti found it difficult to remember all of it, leave alone imagine how she could ever explain it to anyone who hadn't been there to see it all unravel.

'I'm happy to be back,' she said with some semblance of conviction.

Samuel was waiting outside the terminal with the car. He helped Mira into the backseat while Shanti loaded her luggage by herself. Shanti joined Samuel, taking the passenger seat next to him. She automatically shifted the gears for him, a habit they'd never broken after Samuel's hands had healed into their new, mismatched, misshapen forms. They made their way through the traffic jams in town.

Shanti tried, even though she knew her mother was no longer the kind of person with whom she could easily make small talk. They both preferred silence to the strain of attempting social conversation. They had lost the ability for any affectation with each other. So Shanti either said something worthy to her mother or she remained quiet. They shifted into silence as they drove out of the airport. They passed part of a national park. At a distance they saw giraffes grazing on the tops of some sparse underbrush; there was the odd deer—a kudu or an oryx—that scampered along the side of the road. The bougainvillea creepers were in full bloom, showering bursts of colour—fuchsia, violet, amber—at them as they drove past. Some person, society or government had made a new effort to clean up the town: the streets had been swept, the roundabouts offered landscaped pauses of shrubbery and sculpture in the tarmac and gravel that wound itself around the city.

The Sharmas had continued to live in Nairobi through the unsettling times. Insecurity permeated everywhere. It settled under their roofs, it was absorbed through the walls of their homes, it hung in the air they breathed. People had moved out of their large colonial houses. They had left their rolling lawns and manicured gardens to move into collectives. They coalesced into barracks of maisonettes and armies of flats to feel more secure. They formed communities, fortresses and safe havens against the imminent threat of physical danger.

They existed in a state of generalized dread. Things weren't very good. In fact, they were very bad. Their lives comprised a temporary phenomenon. Periods of peace were unusual. News of neighbours and friends who had been looted, carjacked, murdered slipped through their doors and windows and squatted in their homes. The targets were based on the luck of the draw; there was no morality or judgement at play. No one felt immune to the insecurity that cloaked their lives here. They knew they could be next.

—

They drove through the large iron gates of the garden apartments that the Sharmas had been forced to move into after they lost their house. The Sharmas now lived in Muthaiga, an area that had been a posh part of the city since before independence. Their apartment was one of several in two large buildings. The exterior of the apartments was built in the British colonial style with open verandahs. The interiors were spacious and modern. There was a dishwasher in the kitchen, a washing machine and a dryer in the laundry room. The Sharmas' apartment overlooked a garden. It was highly stylized with ornate rosebushes, African lilies, gardenias and other bright flowers that formed geometric patterns on the finely mowed green grass. There was a swimming pool and two tennis courts at the back of the buildings. The servants' quarters were to the side.

Every resident had a keen interest in the goings-on of the other inhabitants in the compound. Whenever possible, they lounged in their verandahs—sipping gin and tonics, vodka mixed with fresh lime juice or whatever the cocktail of the hour and season—and looked out beyond the edges of their own homes, straining to see over the walls into other people's lives. Every day they stood at their window and surveyed the landscape as if they were assessing their own potential, their own future. The common occupation was gathering news. Since official news was so contrived and public news so scarce, strangers, couples, families, neighbours came together to note, list and offer whatever information they had. When all the facts and rumours had been gathered, they weaved their own stories, fictionalizing and fabricating to fill in the holes. It was a grand pastime and they took comfort in the knowledge that they all belonged somewhere in each other's stories.

But the best way to get information was from their servants. They were revered as the finest bearers of news. They had inside information on the private lives of neighbours and a comprehensive view of public information about the government, the corruption, the anarchy that lay ahead; they provided an accurate forecast for when everyone would need to leave this place.

Wairimu was waiting for them at the front door. Shanti's eyes filled up when she saw the housekeeper.

'Aiee, Shanti Sharma. I keep forgetting the woman you are now,' Wairimu exclaimed. 'I do not know if you will fit into the old swimming costume that I kept on your bed in case you wanted to take a jump in the pool.'

Shanti allowed her tiredness to sweep over her as Wairimu folded her into her arms. She saw that her mother was tired too, more than she could ever imagine herself to be, when she looked at Mira's drawn face as she stood leaning heavily on her walking stick.

'A jump in the pool?' Shanti repeated, laughing. 'I think I'll jump into bed instead.'

'Yes, go to bed,' Wairimu clucked. 'I'll bring you some Bournvita and your favourite biscuits that I have baked for you.'

Shanti squeezed Wairimu's hand and said to her mother, 'I think I'll turn in early, ma.'

Mira turned away from the large portrait of Prashant in the hallway to kiss Shanti.

Wairimu fussed over Shanti, tucking her into bed and placing a tray with biscuits and hot cocoa by her side.

'So, what's new?' Shanti asked her.

'Heh, have you seen the Moroccan Mustafa and his family that have moved into 3B?' Wairimu said, sitting down next to Shanti. 'The woman, she is fat. And the man, he goes out every night, drinking and I don't know what. Look, they are leaving just now.' Wairimu drew back the curtains so Shanti could see the couple from her window.

Shellina, a forty-two-year-old Kenyan Muslim businesswoman of south Asian descent, had just moved into the compound with her thirty-five-year-old Moroccan husband. And lots of dependents—her mother, her brother, a baby boy, and another on the way from the looks of it.

They had brought three servants with them, much to Wairimu's disapproval. 'And what will all these servants do in that small apartment? Just eat, talk and move around dust.'

Shanti smiled. Wairimu had always prided herself as the sole keeper of their domain, their independent domestic goddess.

'The Moroccans', as Wairimu referred to them, had moved into the apartment after their own house was broken into the week before.

The burglars had arrived in a white Mercedes Benz. They drove up to the gate and demanded to see the owner of the house. When the askari refused them entry, one of the men slipped out of the car with a machete and slashed him on his neck and arms three times. They left the guard to bleed and glided on towards the house. The leader of the pack, an ordinary civilian like the rest of the group, wore a suit and spoke English fluently and some French as well. The others were bedraggled, seemingly illiterate, and high, most likely on changaa.

'Excuse me, madame,' the leader had said to Shellina when she opened the door to their formidable knocking. 'You will cooperate and your family will not get hurt. But do not worry. We will be fast.'

They first tied up Mustafa and Shellina's brother and made them lie face down on the bare stone floor, then they gagged Shellina and her mother, and finally they turned their attention to emptying the household with smooth efficiency. They knew exactly what to look for.

'The family of your Moroccan husband has given you a good dowry, n'est ce pas?' he asked Shellina softly. 'Bring me the jewels, give me the art, show me where you hide your money. We will also take these carpets and then say kwaheri.'

Shellina, with tears running down her face, obediently followed his instructions. Her Moroccan husband, who had never quite settled into this part of Africa, so south and foreign from the African homeland he knew, didn't react so well. He struck and buffeted the stone floor with his bound body, which only made the men laugh.

Some of the group started to kick him back and forth like a football while they waited for instructions from their leader. 'Karibuni, welcome, African man. Come drink with us,' they taunted.

After three hours of sorting, selecting and looting, they packed the car and made to leave. The leader went to secure the goods in the car. On the way out, the others noticed Shellina's little boy, Khalil, with his sweet berry-brown face framed with soft black curls. The men laughed and said that they should take him away with them. One of them lifted Khalil onto his lap, his breath reeking of alcohol as he leaned in to kiss the young boy. Shellina and her mother struggled to free their hands of the rope tied around them, tears streamed down their faces as they protested through their gags.

The men turned, naturally, on the weaker of the two, the older woman. They punched her in the face. Her lip split and bled. The leader returned to the room, barking orders in Kikuyu. The others scrambled to leave, dropping Khalil, roughly pushing Shellina's mother away, giving Mustafa one last kick on their way out of the door. The sleek Merc slid out of the driveway and in seconds, they were gone.

Shellina and her family moved into the compound the next day. Mustafa took to going out with his Moroccan friends every night and swaggering home, dead drunk, swearing a stream of oaths in Arabic and French against savage black Africa. His was a superior Africa. He came from a place that was refined, cultured, safe. Shellina's mother spent two weeks in hospital, recovering from her bruises and shock. Khalil started to suffer from nightmares and screamed in his sleep. And Shellina continued to run the family business, breaking down into tears whenever she took a break for coffee, a cigarette or lunch.

According to Wairimu, the three servants had slept through the entire episode.

'And what were they dreaming of that they could sleep with all that kelele in the big house? They know. I know it in my heart, they know,' Wairimu proclaimed with one hand on her hip, brandishing the plate of biscuits with the other as she stood at the window and gestured towards the Moroccans.

'Oh, Wairimu, I really hope that isn't true,' Shanti replied. Her stomach twisted into knots as she assessed the parameters of such a deep betrayal, the possibility that members of your own household could orchestrate such a violation and then continue to stay in the house, helping with the move, accepting daily wages, proffering their sympathies as they secretly profited from the theft.

'Eh eh, at least one, he knew for sure,' said Wairimu, still peering through the bedroom window. 'Weh, they are too lucky. No rapes, no guns, no one dead. Sawa, one is there.'

'Well, this is part of the reason why I want to take you and ma away somewhere. We can go to America,' Shanti said, leaning forward.

'Bah. You'll never understand, Shanti. This is our home, for women like your mother and me, whether we like it or not.' Wairimu put the plate back on the tray and folded her arms across her chest. 'Now go to sleep quickly. Your mother won't rest until you do, and we're very tired with all the matata about you coming home.'

'I always knew you would come back,' the housekeeper continued, sniffing in a proprietary manner. 'Maybe not for your mother, but surely for me.'

'Aiy-yai-yai. You'd think I was gone for a year, the way you and ma go on. Why didn't you put an ad in the Mombasa issue of *The Nation,* offering a reward to the first person who managed to capture me from the beach and bring me home?' Shanti said. She turned on her stomach and threw a pillow over her head.

Before she switched off the light, Wairimu looked disapprovingly at Shanti's rump, perfectly outlined in tight denim, the tan line from her bikini bottom peeping out from the four-inch space between the end of her t-shirt and the beginning of her jeans.

Shanti had a dream that night, one that she used to have consistently when she was younger, where she was running from something in some faraway place. In the dream she was about four years old. Her mother was carrying her as she ran through a field. Shanti held onto her tightly. She could see the veins sticking out of her mother's neck, hear her heartbeat pound in her ears. Her mother's cotton sari was drenched in sweat. She could taste a mixture of salt and coconut oil, a taste she knew intimately, the taste that was her mother. Something struck her mother from the back. She lurched forward and Shanti slipped down her lanky frame. Her mother struggled on, with Shanti swinging from her body, her hands still clasped around her neck. Shanti could hear voices close in around them. Her mother tore her body off her and she heard herself scream as she hit the black earth beneath.

Mira heard Shanti crying in her bedroom. She climbed out of bed. It took her too long, she could hear Shanti whimpering the whole time. She groped for her walking stick in the dark, and went to Shanti's room, managing to hurry despite the limp she had now developed. Shanti lay there, her thin body shivering. It broke Mira's heart to see her struggle. Perhaps this was just something that happened to all mothers. All you want is for your children to be happy, but the gods don't always listen to you. Mira was once able to help Shanti. That was what made her feel particularly helpless now. Mira knew that even the most prudent of children were susceptible in ways a mother could not even begin to imagine.

Shanti was too much like her, Mira thought as she looked down at her daughter, and that was Shanti's downfall. Mira always spoke too sharply to Shanti and then berated herself later, but it was only because she saw herself in her daughter. She knew her weaknesses, and that frightened her because, in the end, you cannot protect your own children. Everybody, including Shanti, which was the saddest part, assumed Mira did not care for her. But that wasn't true.

The thing about Mira was that she could not be clever. She had no explanations other than the most simple, no reasons to offer Shanti, nothing to repair the breach that had grown between them. Not even an attempt to veil the walls they'd built around each other.

'They were going to take everything, even you,' Mira wanted to say. 'Why won't you understand? It was the only thing I could do to protect you.'

Shanti was like freshly cut flowers to Mira, even when she looked like this, so distraught, her face a compass for memory. And then, to Mira's relief, Shanti turned on her side and began to sigh instead of weeping. Thank the gods, Mira thought, things are not all lost.

Shanti wept in her sleep as she had wept so many times before. She could not wake from the dream, leave the young girl she had been, even though she wanted to. She couldn't turn away from the sadness. When Wairimu shook her awake, Shanti opened her eyes, her dream still vivid. Wairimu's face was filled with concern.

'Come, Shanti. It's time to get up. Leave those spirits of the dark,' she said, shaking her head. 'Weh, they are too bad.'

Death was attendant. Shanti could almost see the blood on the walls of her room. Her life seemed to be in suspension. She watched Wairimu standing by her bed. Shanti marvelled at Wairimu's calm acceptance of the extraordinary, her passive compliance with the victory of chaos over order, things that Wairimu thought were a rebuke from the heavens, like natural disasters, death from unknown causes and inexplicable dreams.

'Wake up quickly. I've brought your tea. Your mother sent me. She does not like to hear you cry,' Wairimu said in a matter-of-fact way as she drew back the curtains.

Shanti went to her mother's room, still in her nightie, the cup of tea in her hand. A woman stood next to Mira's bed, preparing to begin her massage. Mira looked up at Shanti and smiled weakly. Something resembling guilt passed over her face. Shanti considered it for a moment and then let it go.

'You didn't sleep well, darling,' Mira said. 'Mercilene will give you a massage. You'll feel better.'

'No, thanks,' Shanti replied.

Shanti sat at the edge of Mira's bed and watched the gardener who doubled up as the compound's medicine woman when the residents couldn't afford an actual doctor. She was known as a witch doctor or a charlatan, depending on how you felt about her remedies. Mercilene ministered oil all over Mira's small body and started to massage her soft skin, stroking it, bringing relief to some of the pain Mira had developed lying in bed all day.

Shanti and Mira sat in subdued silence all morning. Shanti would have placated her mother if she knew what to say; told her it wasn't her fault, if only her heart would let her. Shanti would have closed the space between them, the black expanse that became larger whenever she came too close. She would have embraced her mother and told her they need never take it up again, if only she knew how.

Instead, Shanti thought about a time when her father was still alive. They had driven out of the city to Tsavo National Park on the morning of the solar eclipse. Prashant parked his car in the middle of the plains. He turned to the back seat and gave Shanti cardboard sunglasses to protect her eyes.

'What am I supposed to do with these?' Shanti asked.

'Put them on, what else?' her father replied with a laugh.

Mira leaned towards Shanti and whispered, 'The shadow planets are about to swallow the sun. Look into that darkness and you will see the journey of your soul.'

Shanti remembered solemnly putting on the paper glasses, secretly doubting the ability of such a whimsical accessory to provide any sort of telescopic penetration into her being.

They settled back to watch the eclipse, marvelling at the birds that flocked to their nests as the sky darkened behind the trees that brushed against each other in the light breeze. Giraffes, zebras, bushbucks galloped across the plains, collecting their young and scurrying behind bushes, thinking that night had come early. Her father had held her mother's hand as they watched the eclipse obscure the vast African sky.

The doorbell rang and Shanti stood up quickly, explaining that Mariella had come over to study. She ran to the door.

'Hello, Hap-ee-ness!' Mariella deliberately cooed at Shanti as she slid around Wairimu, who had opened the door. The attempt was clumsy since Mariella was as tall as Wairimu, but she managed to squeeze past the older woman, who was much heavier than her.

'Hello, Boo-ti-fool!' Shanti said, avoiding looking at Wairimu as she cooed back at her friend. 'Let's go for a swim. I mean, let's take our books to the pool and study there.'

'The first one to jump into the pool will kiss Sebu!' Mariella shouted as the two of them ran down the length of the garden, past the tennis courts towards the swimming pool.

Partly because of the searing stone path under her feet, partly because of the redness that blossomed over her skin whenever Mariella mentioned Sebu, Shanti reached the edge of the pool first. She jumped into the water, thinking again how unfair it was that her skin was lighter and thinner than her friend's, and that she had a friend who felt so free to notice and openly comment about everything and everyone associated with her. The cold water engulfing her as she jumped into the pool was a relief.

Shanti felt some of the edges of her nightmare that had remained with her through the morning ease away. As she dove deep underwater, she tried to sort through the images that had resurfaced into her consciousness. She tried to distinguish dream from memory. It was still in a muddle, still a mystery to her. She climbed out of the pool at the other end, feeling as if her life was elsewhere. The red earth of Africa was familiar but it reminded her of something else: a place where there was blood in the air, draining into the earth. A memory from a different time, a different continent even. And then, just as recognition hovered over her, as if preparing to settle down on her, it slipped away and she lost her chance of attaining clarity as the rich, moist African mud came into focus under a very blue sky and a bright sun.

'You could have waited for me. Honestly, girl, where are your manners?' said Mariella, climbing out of the pool after she had swum its entire length. 'Or were you afraid I was going to have sex with your precious Sebu if I caught up?'

Shanti didn't answer. She squinted, admiring the geometry of the sunlight as it skimmed over the pool. Shanti bent forward to shake the water out of her hair and the residue of memory along with it. Her long black hair hung like a curtain over her body, casting a shadow on the taut muscles of her thighs. She heard Mariella giggle before she felt a sharp nudge in her upside-down torso.

'Ouch. Don't do that,' she said, straightening up, letting her hair cascade heavily down her back. She looked in the direction Mariella pointed and saw a man standing by the gate of the pool area under the archway of the golden shower creeper. He was appraising their bodies in what felt more like a scientific manner than anything else.

Shanti walked up to him and said briskly, 'May I help you?'

The man was much taller than Shanti and she didn't like the fact that she had to tilt her face to meet his eyes. She felt that she was at a disadvantage because she was barefoot and had only a towel wrapped around her wet bathing suit.

The man smiled self-consciously and extended his right hand. 'Your mother sent me down here to meet you. I'm Simon Lindsay, your new physics teacher.'

Shanti was taken off guard. She realized she had been staring at him and quickly thrust her wet hand into his to make up for the long pause. The man let his hand stay there as if he were not sure what to do now.

'When we complained about Mr Pinto playing tennis outside instead of teaching us, Sister Josephine said that girls can't do physics, anyway,' Mariella informed him. She'd walked up to Shanti and the man, still wearing her wet bathing suit without wrapping a towel around herself.

'Well, that's why Sister Thomas Aquinas fired him, hired me and reprimanded Sister Josephine when she learned about what Mr Pinto did,' Simon replied, briefly resting his eyes on Mariella's face before turning back to Shanti. 'Your headmistress knows very well that girls can do physics.'

'I would like to know what you're doing on my property, Mr Lindsay,' Shanti said quickly.

The man appeared taken aback for a moment and then quickly looked down. He wiped his hand on his trousers deliberately.

'Your mother's asked me to tutor you on Saturday afternoons. We spoke when she called the school a few weeks ago while I was managing the office. Sister Thomas Aquinas was away at Mass. You know, she called to confirm that your school trip had indeed been extended by two weeks.'

Shanti faltered. He had played a trump card.

'Look, Mr Lindsay, I need some notice about these things. And if I have to take extra tuitions, Mariella has to take them with me.' She squared her shoulders as she edged closer to her friend.

'Ah, well. I would suggest that the best thing for you to do is to speak with your mother,' he said, punctuating his words with pauses as if he were choosing them carefully. 'And by the way, if you're not going to call me by my first name, it's Doctor Lindsay, not Mister. I'm only here for a couple of months on a break from the medical camps at the border and offered to volunteer at the mission schools.'

Shanti and Mariella watched him as he walked up the grey flagstones back to the apartment buildings.

'Wow! Loreto Convent Kilimani is turning into an a-ca-demee, hiring doctors and what not,' Mariella said in a singsong voice. 'It's good, anyway. Otherwise we'll end up like that other jua kali Loreto you went to before. What was its name?'

'Loreto Hill Valley,' Shanti replied.

'Eh, what a crazy name for a crazy school. They made you become a Christian there so you could stay on, right? Now you can remain a heathen like me at Kili and still benefit from a convent ed-you-ca-shon.'

'We're not heathens,' Shanti said, happy to have something to be angry about. 'You're Protestant and I'm Hindu.'

'Then why don't you spend time with the muhindi clan in school, and me with my Protestant Mwa-Afrikans? You and me, we will always be heathens, my friend. Total outcasts. The kid of a Ugandan politician who has left his children in Kenya as if they are still refugees and the kid of a crazy muhindi mother with no father or any other relatives to speak of,' Mariella declared as she slung an arm around Shanti's shoulders.

Shanti shrugged her arm off, feeling betrayed at Mariella's casual declaration about her family.

'What are you so fussed about, anyway?' Mariella continued. 'Are you afraid Sebu is not a fellow heathen or something? Some Ethiopians aren't Catholic either, you know.'

'Sebu doesn't know I exist.'

'We'll have to fix that by climbing over the gate to Saints more often. Too bad the boys have lunch break during physics. Mistah, I mean, Daktari Lindsay will be disappointed when we don't show up for class.'

'We're not going to go over to the boys' school, Mariella. We'll get caught.' Shanti handed Mariella a towel to wrap around herself so they could go back to the apartment.

'Aati, where is your sense of ad-ven-cha?' Mariella sighed. 'Or does Sebu have competition now?'

Shanti didn't reply as they began to walk back in the stillness of the afternoon.

'If you're going to get an-y-bod-ee to notice you, you have to learn to work *it*,' said Mariella, pulling off her towel and sashaying in front of Shanti. 'As if you're a Baganda, Ugandan, proper prime time lay-dee. Like yours truly.'

Shanti wrapped the towel around Mariella as they crossed the courtyard to the kitchen.

Shanti and Mariella returned to find Mira and Lata sitting out on the verandah. Lata was telling Mira the latest gossip. She lingered over each story as though her podgy, bejewelled fingers held a pot of treasure, embellishing each word as if she were unwrapping sweets for Mira. It was the usual mixed bag of news.

Meena's husband Yusuf, the furniture-maker, was having an affair with the Finnish ambassador's wife whom he met while furnishing their embassy house; Selina's daughter Raissa, who lived in Geneva, was divorcing her husband, thereby ruining the second marriage arranged for her (rumour had it she was having an affair with her sister-in-law); Daniel Kariuki, a cabinet minister, had his privileges revoked at the Muthaiga Golf Club because he became very drunk one evening and started to practise his chipping in the clubhouse, pitching golf balls at various members' heads in the process; the government had set up an official anti-corruption unit. Lata's conversation was filled with self-aggrandizing stories, sprinkled with slights against Mira and the condition of her household.

'Hai, my teeth hurt so much, trying to chew on these hard biscuits, and this tea is so weak. It's no wonder you're looking so sick, Mira,' Lata said. 'Lucky for me, I still get invited to all the important parties. I just had tea at the High Commission before coming to see you, and the Deputy High Commissioner's wife said I must call the High Commissioner's doctor if I ever feel the least bit under the weather. And their tea is always so nice and smooth—pure Darjeeling, you know. They served all kinds of bhajias—bondas, samosas, you name it. You should really let your woman go and get someone who won't serve guests these stale biscuits.'

Wairimu and Shanti rolled their eyes at each other as the housekeeper finished serving tea and left the room.

'Shanti, my darling,' Lata gushed as she stood up. 'My god, you've grown up!'

Lata's gold bangles jingled as she put her arms around Shanti's waist. Shanti was smothered in her sweet perfume as Lata kissed the space between her cheek and shoulder. Her shrewd gaze quickly swept over Shanti.

'You look a shade darker every time I see you,' she said.

'Hello, Lata aunty,' Shanti replied, her eyes sombre, willing Lata to calm down. 'We just came back from the coast. It was a school trip. Mariella got a tan, too. Do you know my friend, Mariella?'

Mariella bowed in front of Lata and Mira and took one of Lata's chubby hands in her own, shaking it vigorously. Lata let her arm drop to her side, not knowing what to do. Shanti couldn't help covering her face with her towel as she tried to stop her laughter.

'Mira, I don't understand these young people today,' Lata turned back to Mira. 'Can you believe Ash has an African woman living with him now? After all we've done for him, he's threatening to marry this girl who works with him at Oxfam. And we can't even say anything publicly because she's a judge's daughter. Mohanji works with her father.'

'Oh, Ash is still here,' Mira said vaguely.

'Honestly, what is poor Mohanji supposed to do? Hold a half-kaala baby in his lap with hair like tight wires on its head and hear it call him Dadaji?'

'That might do Mohan uncle some good, actually,' Shanti declared.

'It is nice to have Lata visit me,' said Mira quickly, sensing that her daughter was about to face off with her friend.

'After such a long time!' Lata said, ignoring Shanti. 'I never see you now that you've made these new friends in the compound. Who was it that even told you about this apartment when you lost your house?'

'It was you,' Shanti said before her mother could answer. The woman was a cartoon.

'And I must thank you for that, Lata,' Mira said evenly, glancing at Shanti.

It was like some sort of game with these women. Shanti had her limits. She shrugged her shoulders and made an excuse to return indoors. She dragged away Mariella, who had helped herself in the meantime to the plate of crisps and biscuits that had been set out by Wairimu for Lata to have with her tea.

—

As Shanti waited for Lata to leave, she and Mariella skulked around Mira's room like children confined in detention. Unlike her flamboyant friend, Mira had simple tastes. Her bedroom was stark, all clean lines and bare surfaces. There were no pictures on the cream walls, there was a bed and a dressing table made of solid oak, a hand-woven Rajasthani razai with tiny yellow flowers and blue leaves scattered all over it, and cheery yellow curtains hanging over the large window. Without Mira in it, it looked like any ordinary bedroom, designed to be primarily inhabited at night.

Mariella went up to the dressing table and casually looked through Mira's things. She chose a lipstick from the few Mira still had, lying unused in one of the drawers. Mariella pressed her lips together after she put on the lipstick, making sure the colour had spread evenly.

Shanti envied Mariella's self-confidence. Mariella had the kind of looks men found beautiful in this part of the world, with her olive-coloured skin and high cheekbones, her long, toned legs and tapering neck. Shanti thought Mariella was of mixed race when she met her during her first week at her new school but Mariella had informed her, without Shanti asking, that she had some Portuguese blood in her ancestral lineage, which was why she was lighter than most African girls and had the last name 'Dagama'. 'You mean you're part Goan,' one of the other girls had said, laughing. 'That is why you are trying to be best friends with a muhindi.' Mariella had jabbed her finger in the girl's face and replied, 'Aati, learn your history. Vas-co-da-ga-ma was Por-cha-geez.' Shanti and Mariella began to have lunch on their own at the far end of the school field after that, leaving the other girls to sit on the benches under the trees near the classrooms, each narrow plank of wood equably populated by girls of the same race.

Shanti turned away from Mariella, who was still looking at her own reflection in the mirror. She felt too insignificant if she stared at her friend for long.

Mira had a collection of Ganeshas on the dressing table. There were various forms of the little god of luck, the destroyer of all obstacles, with his potbelly and elephant head. Carved in marble, glass, copper and jade, he rested in his traditional seated pose, his legs crossed, his right ankle resting on his left heel, one palm raised in a benevolent gesture. There were little silver and brass figures of Ganesha as a baby, crawling on all fours, an arm and a leg sprawled out, as if reaching for a treat. It would have to be a stack of laddoos, Ganesha and Shanti agreed, as she filled in the imaginary pyramid of sweetmeats, those orbs of spangled gold, for him, completing the picture.

'Does that woman not know how to shake hands or something?' Mariella asked Shanti as she put away the lipstick and continued to go through Mira's things.

'It's not really our custom for children to bow in front of adults and shake their hands,' Shanti replied. 'I'm sorry you had to listen to all that. She's so racist!'

Mariella lifted her shoulders slightly, not giving Lata the importance of a full blown shrug. 'I'm sure the girl's side is having the same conversations. Which Kenyan parents want their daughter to marry a skinny Indian guy when they can get a big, lion-hearted African man?' Mariella let out a roar and threw her arms around Shanti.

'Yes, what is going on here?' Wairimu said, walking straight into Mira's bedroom.

Shanti unwrapped Mariella's arms from her body.

'Mariella, your driver is here.' Wairimu gestured at Mariella, her eyes fixed on Shanti.

'He is not my dry-vah, he is my brah-dah,' Mariella said.

Shanti was not sure if Mariella was making fun of Wairimu's English or falling into their joking pronunciations. She quickly went to the hallway to get Mariella her bag which held her wet swimsuit and untouched school books.

At the front door, Mariella leaned forward and clapped her hands over Wairimu's ears so that the two of them were face to face. She gave Wairimu a loud kiss on each cheek. Wairimu stepped backwards, stunned.

'It is not the muhindi's custom for children to shake hands,' Mariella explained to her. 'When in Lome, do as the Loh-mans.' Mariella had pronounced her r's like l's just as Wairimu often did when she spoke English.

'That girl is loose,' Wairimu said, following Shanti as she went back to her room. 'She has a loose mouth and a loose walk.'

'She's my best friend,' said Shanti.

'She comes from a bad family.'

'Her parents were political refugees here! Her father is now helping Museveni build back that country after Idi Amin and Obote destroyed it! Her mother is an educated businesswoman!'

'So what? Her mother comes to Nairobi to buy things to sell in her shop in Kampala and she does not even stop to say hello to her children who live on their own in a house with a servant they order around. Her father is now a big man, hungry, hungry all the time to feed his own stomach. What kinds of parents are these that they are only interested in power and money?'

'And how are they so different from you, with your big big ideas of buying a duka in town and your own house in your village?'

Wairimu drew back. She decided not to reply, turned on her heel and walked out of Shanti's room.

They were always like this now, Shanti and Wairimu, like two disgruntled cats in search of a satisfying spat.

15

SHANTI COULD FEEL THE strains of excitement from the girls hovering around the notice that Simon had put up on the board outside Sister Thomas Aquinas's office, all the way at the end of the school field where she and Mariella were lying under the scant shade offered by the thorn trees, smoking cigarettes. The wind seemed to contain this excitement as it curled itself around the slim lime-green trunks, shaving the bark of its felt covering. The bleached white shirts of their school uniforms were stained yellow as the wind shook the trees. Shanti leaned into the sighing wind, wishing it would take her away with it.

'You don't have to worry,' Mariella said, noticing Shanti's wistful glances towards the school building. 'We're already on the team.'

'How do you know?' Shanti asked.

'St Joseph's has the power over anything they do with their sister school. The five boys are from the Saints' hockey team and Simon told them they could pick five girls so that all five boys can play in this inter-school hockey competition,' Mariella explained. 'My brother is on the team and I already bribed him so he would convince the boys to pick us. Simon favours you, anyway, so our places are secured.'

'We don't even have hockey sticks,' Shanti said, trying to remain skeptical, though she could already feel the excitement race over her skin, causing her to shiver a little.

'The schools will provide. It's not much. Most of the boys own their own equipment. My parents give my brothers whatever amount they ask for sports. It's not fair, I tell you,' Mariella said, stubbing out her cigarette on the parched wild grass they were sitting on. 'Sebu's hockey stick looks as if it is attached to his body, the way he walks around, waving it in the air like a machete. My brother says that boy will kill himself if he doesn't become sports prefect next year.'

'What did you have to bribe your brother with this time?' Shanti asked. She kept her head down as she started to dig a hole in the ground so she could bury their cigarette stubs, hoping Mariella could not see her face after the mention of Sebu.

'A pack of cigarettes and some other gifts I'm too modest to talk to you about,' Mariella said casually. She changed the subject. 'Let's go tell Simon we're already on the team. He's always so happ-ee to see his cue-tee Shan-tee.'

They found Simon on the hockey pitch that was shared by both missionary schools but that was technically on the boys' school property, just beyond the low, rusty gate. Simon was standing in the middle of the pitch with a group of boys, absorbed in concentration as he drew defence strategies in the mud with a hockey stick.

Mariella turned the metal tap near the gate and rubbed water over her legs to make them look shiny. She asked Shanti to do the same but Shanti demurred. She was sure no one would be looking at her with Mariella standing by her side. Mariella walked up to the group with Shanti following a few steps behind. They were careful to cross from the part of the pitch that didn't have any chalk lines drawn on it. Their black leather pumps and white socks were coated in red dust by the time they reached the centre of the pitch.

'Two of our fellow players approach,' Simon said, grinning at the girls. 'I hear you've already made the team.'

'We want to know when practice begins,' Mariella said, jutting out her hip and sending sidelong glances to each of the boys.

'Aati, we do not need to practise with them. The girls just have to show up and stand on the pitch, holding sticks.'

This was the first time Shanti had heard Sebu speak. His accent was rougher than she had imagined. She looked towards him and found that he was looking directly at her. She quickly looked away. Sebu waved his hockey stick in the air as he spoke. His dark brown curls were cropped close to his tan-coloured skin. His light blue school shirt was open at the collar, revealing a necklace of thinly sliced cowrie strung together, the white shells glinted as they rested against his muscular neck.

'Now, what did I tell you?' Simon turned to the boys. 'You can only play in this tournament against the international schools if the team includes girls.'

'Coach, practices were not part of the deal,' Sebu said. He positioned his stick on the ground and hit a make-believe hockey ball across the pitch. 'You've already made me shed half my team.'

Shanti hadn't realized that Sebu was the captain.

'We will chapaa the mzungus anyway,' one of the boys shouted, receiving cheers from the rest. 'We will beat them even though you have halved us, coach.'

Mariella stared at her brother, Milo, but he refused to acknowledge her. She made a face at him and turned to leave. Shanti followed her.

'Just remember to show up at the match and bring the other three girls with you,' Sebu shouted after them.

'Do you see how their shoes have spoilt the pitch? Weh-weh,' another boy said, shaking his head in disgust, eliciting agreement from the rest.

'You should stick to teaching us sports and the girls physics, coach,' another one added, and was rewarded with laughter from his audience.

'Shanti, Mariella.' Simon followed them. 'Just make sure you select hockey during your P.E. time so you're able to practise, okay?'

'Okay, Dr Lindsay—or is it coach?' Mariella shouted without turning around. 'Thanks a lot, coach.'

Shanti looked back and Simon smiled at her before he went back to join the boys who had already re-immersed themselves in their drawings on the ground.

—

Shanti came home from school just as Flip was entering their apartment. She was an artist who lived in one of the flats in the second building. She had started to visit Mira every alternate day of the week.

'I come bearing adornments,' Flip declared as she bounced into Mira's bedroom, dangling brightly dyed pieces of papier-mâché from her short spiky hair.

'Adornments?' Mira asked, a delighted smile playing on her lips as if she were still a young girl.

They laughed together. Flip and Mira shared the same sense of the absurd. Mira's friend was in her fifties. She was petite, she couldn't have been more than five feet. A close crop of silver hair barely covered her head. She was wiry and had a seemingly boundless store of energy. Her exuberance was tempered by her perpetually sorrowful eyes—the only indication of the lonely void she seemed unable to fill.

Flip was an unplanned child, conceived in error by members of different classes and entirely different manners of living, who were then forced to spend the rest of their lives together, tied by the bonds of matrimony, the presence of a child a constant reminder of their misjudgement in a moment of casual intimacy. Flip's parents had been forced to get married by their families, though neither acquired any joy from this union.

In Nairobi, where she had intended to live with her relatives during her time in Africa, Flip's mother had played tennis and gone horseback riding. She had participated in theatrical skits at the club. Flip's mother was the sort of young woman who had spent afternoons in Nairobi painting still-life in the garden, a glass of iced Pimm's by her side. She had been happy living in the capital, this woman who found that she was to spend the rest of her life on an African farm because of an impropriety she could not undo. Both Flip's parents were flabbergasted that their extemporaneous intimacy, one that was never intended to lead to something weighty, ended in Flip's father, a white settler, taking her mother whom he had met during one of his trips to Nairobi, back to his farm.

Throughout the period of her pregnancy, Flip's mother was ill. The labour was difficult. After Flip's birth, her mother was so exhausted she didn't want to see her baby. When the physician inquired about the baby's name and found there wasn't one, he looked down at the child in his arms and murmured, 'Flippa.' Probably because Flip had kicked out so much during her birth, turning this way and that. Or perhaps he had meant to say 'Philippa', but 'Flippa' stuck, initially because no one took the time to change it, and later because Flip clung to it desperately, as a reminder both of the first person who had acknowledged her existence and of her mother's neglect of her emergence into this world.

After the birth, Flip's mother settled into a depression and continued to barely acknowledge the presence of her daughter. She had milk but refused to feed so Flip was bottle-fed from the start, drinking cow's milk from her father's farm. Flip became very sick, probably because no one bothered to check the milk, collected by the Maasai workers on the farm and likely mixed with unboiled water and cow's blood as was the usual practice so there'd be enough for everyone to share.

Flip's mother felt she had nothing in common with her neighbours; she belonged in Nairobi, after all. She did not join in the stories about the fickleness of Africa, how nothing was as it first appeared—an honest farmhand turned out to be a cheating scoundrel; a log naively sat on, a writhing python.

She battled fervidly against her life there for a while. She would get dressed in elaborate frocks that she had designed and wear handmade wigs that were not intended to fit in with the practical existence in which she was now immersed. Her own hair was red and curly, and over it she would sheath herself with a wig made of tin foil and steel wool or a cap of guinea fowl feathers and tinsel that made her seem to be impersonating, in very amateur fashion, a bellicose lead in a grand opera. Her neighbours started to refer to her as 'the English Ma'am', not because her English blood was more perceptible than their own, but because her enunciation had a feigned BBC-World-Service-radio quality to it.

Soon afterwards, Flip's mother complained of a hundred ailments and went back to bed. But an afflicted patrician lady stranded in the African bundu wasn't all Flip knew of her mother. Her bedsheets became a canvas upon which she let Flip paint her first portraits. Flip's mother would ask her daughter to draw a picture of her dancing in a ballroom, or playing cards and smoking after dinner, or chatting with friends at a cocktail party. Flip, who had no knowledge of the city life, had to use her imagination, conjuring pictures that would please and flatter her mother. Flip's mother showed her how to perceive things differently from how they first appear. It was she who introduced Flip to the rest of the world, a world into which Flip escaped, from her mother and from the rest of the life that comprised her home.

Flip came to see Mira every other afternoon in the week. She brought good cheer, in the form of art she created for Mira the day before each visit. It was a random assortment of garish primary colours in the guise of tie-and-dye fabric, patches of batik and silk screens.

'Tell me, my darling,' Flip said to Shanti, 'about that gorgeous young man who was ogling you at the pool the other day?'

'There's not much to tell, Flip.'

'Men and women are just like dogs,' Flip declared. 'We pretend to bare our teeth while we're sneakily sniffing out each other's bottoms.'

Mira and her friend collapsed into peals of laughter until tears streamed down their faces.

Flip was entirely odd if not dangerously close to insane, Shanti decided. She watched her prance about Mira's barely furnished room, pausing to stand on her head (to centre herself, she explained to Shanti) at herky-jerky pauses in her frenzied jig. Mira delighted in her visits. It was as if Flip were her younger sister, the light-hearted maverick she never quite dared to be.

Carol Wijenje joined Mira and Flip in the evening after she returned from work. She was a professor at Nairobi University. Carol and her husband also lived in the compound. Carol was tall, reserved and always impeccably dressed in custom-made suits and stilettos, her hair braided and swept off her face in a high bun. Carol and Shanti had become friends. She was graceful with Shanti about Mira's condition, always careful not to show her distress at Mira's visible deterioration while she inquired if she could do anything to enhance Mira's comfort. She was ever gainfully occupying herself, changing the flowers in Mira's room with a fresh bouquet, smoothing down Mira's bedspread and tucking in the edges at the foot of the bed, sorting piles of books that she had borrowed from the British Council library on Mira's behalf. Carol talked to Mira with an honesty and inspiration that Shanti herself was unable to muster.

Carol's father was a politician, close to the 'Great Men of Africa' who had fought for the continent's emancipation. As a young man, he had struggled side by side with men like Kenyatta, Nyerere and Kaunda in the pursuit for independence from their British colonizers. Older now, he profited from the theft of their nations' bounty. Carol's mother had stood by him during the afflicted times of the Mau Mau Revolution. Back then, she was his equal, his compatriot in their struggle for Kenya's independence. She shared in his dreams for the country's freedom and his own political success. When Kenya gained independence in 1963, Carol's father was elected to lead his constituency. After Jomo Kenyatta died in 1978 and Daniel Arap Moi succeeded him, there was a scramble for political power which ended in Carol's father gaining a seat in parliament.

As his political prominence grew, so did his appetite for personal dominion. He acquired numerous properties and additional wives. Carol's mother, frail of health by then, receded into the shadows of Carol's childhood home. She finally decided to live in western Kenya, away from her husband's political reach and the shifting powers in his household. Carol's father's second wife assumed the role of the keeper of his home. She kept watch over his charge, his children and his possessions.

It was a severe home. Carol's father ruled his household with the cane. Carol spoke of her father with the admiration due to him for his role in the country's struggle for independence, but Shanti never heard her speak of him with love. Carol treated her mother like a member of her extended family from the village, an annual intruder into her urban existence, one she had to endure on occasion. There was no regard for the youthful stepmother, who was quiet and submissive and could not tolerate the children from her husband's first wife.

Mira and Carol shared a similar context in different circumstances. When her stepmother wearied of trying to account for the old politician's children, much like Mira, Carol was sent away to a Loreto Convent boarding school. Carol was good at her studies. She vowed to make a contribution to the development of Kenya, to break the cycle of corruption perpetuated by her father and his associates. Carol refused to go abroad for college and went to Nairobi University to earn her PhD instead. She found herself surrounded by young men and women who did not have the same privileges and education as her. They resented her for it, ridiculing her city-bred manners and effete attitudes. They taunted her because she bore her father's name.

During her time at university, she met another student, an African man of more modest means than herself. He would tell anyone who stopped to listen, about how his country had failed him, how angry he was at the inescapable malfeasance sewn into every aspect of existence in his country, how no Kenyan had witnessed an honest election since the country's independence. Carol was moved by his conviction, by the disappointment he felt towards the men who had fought for independence and then squandered the very ideals for which they had sacrificed everything—towards men like her father. Carol fell in love with him. She married him and decided to set aside her own desires for initiating change within the government in order to support his ambitions. She decided to enter academia while her husband became a politician.

'Do you think I made a mistake?' Carol asked Mira. 'I sometimes worry that I've followed in my mother's footsteps and I will slowly fade into the background while my husband dishonours the values we once cherished so he can continue his political career.'

'No, I don't think so,' Mira replied. 'Times have changed. We all have other, fairer alternatives available to us. Political success does not necessarily involve a compromise of personal morals any more.'

Shanti wondered at her mother's ingenuousness. She was more skeptical about the individual motivations of anyone interested in pursuing a political career in this part of the world. As she went to the kitchen to tell Wairimu that Mira's friends would be staying for dinner, she deliberated over Carol's decision, questioning whether Carol had made the error of repeating history—her mother's own life story—by subordinating her own ambitions for the particular aspirations of her husband.

'And what am I supposed to make for them with no advance notice?' Wairimu asked Shanti.

'It doesn't matter. I'm not that hungry, just give them whatever you've made for ma and me,' Shanti said, placating the housekeeper. 'Why are you so fussed, anyway?'

'Fussed? Me? Why doesn't that mzungu fuss over your mother and take her out to restaurants, like she takes her own house boy, instead of expecting me to cook for her?' Wairimu retorted.

'The mzungus do that for special occasions with their servants, Wairimu,' Shanti said mildly. 'You know that.'

'I know that it is patronage, that is what I know,' Wairimu said. 'We are not equal for them. They do not treat us as equals. Then one night they embarrass us by taking us to a place we do not belong, and prove to themselves that we are not equal. Me, I do not like your mother's new friends and I do not like your new friend, Shanti.'

'Mariella is not my new friend,' Shanti replied, walking out of the kitchen, tired of returning to the same conversation again and again. 'She's my only friend.'

—

Wairimu had a personal reason for being pricklier than her usual generous self. She was upset with Mira. Wairimu had asked Mira for a loan earlier that morning.

'What?' Mira had exclaimed, 'What happened to the 20,000 shillings I gave you to build your house last month. Anyway, you know my policy on loans.'

Mira refused to give loans to her servants. She felt it exacerbated the feelings of resentment servants had towards their employers. Through past experience she had learned that with each instalment of the loan repayment, the hostility towards her increased. She had discovered that servants resented the fact that she actually collected money from them, even though it was the repayment of an interest-free loan. They failed to see or ignored the fact that she actually lost money from the transaction. But the overall value lost was greater than a bad business deal. She felt she lost their goodwill. So in the face of a multitude of requests for loans from her servants, she had resorted to giving them the money instead. She hoped it would alleviate the negative residue that was ironed into the laundry and stirred into their meals whenever a servant was faced with the prospect of making a loan repayment.

Mira had turned a business transaction into a personal peace offering. But since most servants had the need for vast amounts of money due to the scores of marriages, initiation ceremonies, illnesses and deaths that befell their family members—often all on the same family member multiple times she had to be discerning about these gifts.

In this part of the world, if you left your village to seek work in town, you automatically became the family breadwinner, the hero, the beloved, regardless of your age, gender or status in the hierarchical extended family structure. So Wairimu and Samuel frequently came to Mira, seeking tranches of money, and the household would be in turmoil while Mira expelled lectures, exclaimed her irritation, and the person in question grovelled, whined and sulked, until no one could stand living under the same roof with these shenanigans and a deal was struck, a gift endowed.

16

SHANTI SAT IN THE garden one Saturday afternoon, underneath the pepper tree behind the two blocks of flats, working on a problem Simon had given her from an old Cambridge GCE exam paper. Mariella had abandoned it fifteen minutes ago, declaring that she needed a short swim to lodge the required equation out of her memory and onto her exercise-book. Light arched through the knobby branches and reflected off the large spade-like leaves of the anthuriums on the ground, the orange flowers looked like tongues of fire lit by the sun.

Simon slung his blazer over his shoulder as he leaned against the pepper tree, watching Shanti write out her answer.

'Here,' Shanti said, throwing the soft-cover exercise-book on the ground in his direction. 'Can I go join Mariella now?'

'Wait, Shanti,' Simon replied. He lowered himself on the grass next to Shanti, letting his eyes slide over her thin body under her white cotton sundress. Shanti knew everyone had noticed she had lost weight.

'How are you?' Simon asked.

'Oh, fine. Mariella and I are playing hockey during P.E. every week. We won't embarrass you,' Shanti replied.

'Actually, I was asking how you are, Shanti.' He paused. 'I know about the dreams.'

'Wairimu told me,' he explained when he saw Shanti look away, preparing to shut down. 'I know none of this is easy for you. You should let me prescribe something for your bedtime,' he added with a smile. 'Even if it is only chamomile tea.'

'What a lovely remedy,' Shanti said. 'I wish the prescriptions the doctor gives my mother were that simple.'

'I can explain any of the medication she's taking if you give me the names,' Simon offered.

'I don't think there's much point, really,' she said in a quieter voice. 'Everyone says the headaches and now this problem with her leg is either imaginary or because she spends so much time in bed.'

They sat on the grass in the calm reserve of the afternoon sun. Shanti's eyes followed two weaverbirds as they darted through the golden shower creeper over the archway leading to the pool. The birds tried to suck nectar out of the long tubed flowers as they teetered precariously on the slim stalks and inevitably lost their balance, slipping down the vine. She laughed as the obtuse creatures tried the same feat over and over again. Simon watched her and smiled.

'I join the Museum Society for a bird walk every Sunday morning. I can collect you on my way there tomorrow if you'd like to come along,' he said.

'I'd love to, Simon,' Shanti smiled at him, and then quickly covered her mouth because she'd called him by his first name to his face.

Simon picked Shanti up at seven the next morning in a fairly beaten-up white Range Rover. He remained unperturbed through the rush-hour traffic congestion, deftly steering the four-wheel drive through the random order of the streets. Everywhere Shanti turned, drivers look annoyed, the character of their day seemed set. She rolled up her window and turned inward, inside the car. She made sure her seat belt was secure as she leaned into the seat. Simon glanced at her.

'Nairobi's become a mess, a bulging sprawl completely lacking in urban planning and filled to the brim with all the commotion that comes with disorder,' he said.

The road to the museum was particularly precarious. It was on a steep hill that carried four, sometimes five, lanes of traffic even though it was constructed for merely two. They had to make a sharp right turn into the museum gates, cutting across several lanes of oncoming vehicles.

The museum grounds were an oasis of quiet after the honking vehicles outside. After he parked the car, Simon opened up the hatchback and filled up his rucksack for the walk. He packed two sets of binoculars, a bird book, a first-aid kit, a flask of tea and a packet of biscuits.

'Gosh, I feel as if we're off on a safari,' Shanti said.

Simon laughed. 'It's best to be prepared.'

He eyed her loafers. Shanti noticed a pair of tennis shoes in a corner of the boot. They looked about her size.

'What did you think I'd be wearing—high heels?' she asked him, her eyebrows arched.

'No, that's not it.' He shrugged. 'I just thought you mightn't have brought walking shoes with you.'

'Who do they belong to, anyway?' The slur of suspicion in her voice startled her. 'May I ask?'

'My sister left them here on her last visit from London,' Simon said. 'I don't have a wife or girlfriend locked away in a cupboard somewhere.'

'No, no. That's not what I meant to imply in any way,' she explained quickly, feeling herself blush.

A collection of the city's bird-watchers had gathered near the steps of the museum. There were a few expatriate wives, an old British couple and some students of ornithology. A short man with large watery eyes and a rotund middle stood before them. He was balding but had an enormous shock of hair jutting out from the back of his skull. His long triangular nose in front balanced out the protrusion of feathery hair. If he were a bird, he would have to be a Hamerkop. Shanti felt pleased with her adroit analogy.

He twitched his head from side to side as he spoke.

'Right-o, folks. I thought it would be quite a lot of fun if we drove to the Ngong race course this morning. We're not going to the derby, of course,' he added hastily. 'It's unfortunate the betting office is shut this morning.'

There was a chorus of appreciative laughter.

'But there'll be plenty of sport, no doubt, in the woods on the property there.'

The Hamerkop, whose name was Bill Jones, distributed the walkers among the drivers. Simon offered to give the three university students a lift. They sat in the back and flipped eagerly through their bird books. Simon spoke to them in Kiswahili. They had just returned from a weekend field trip to Lake Baringo where they had sighted 450 species of birds in one day. Shanti was impressed by the number. Spurred on by her awe, the students showed her pictures of some of the birds they had identified there. Simon quickly explained which birds were rare so that Shanti could express suitable appreciation. Pale and dark phase gabar goshawk, paradise flycatchers, African fish eagles, Marabou storks, shikra and white-faced scops owls were among the regular sightings while some of the less common birds they saw included Hemprich's hornbill along the cliffs, the African darter and the African skimmer.

Shanti's flimsy acquaintance with bird-watching did not help her on this excursion. Bill Jones, the leader of the gaggle, delighted at the prospect of a new addition to his weekly bird walks, tucked Shanti's arm into his and dragged her from bush to tree, pointing out what seemed like an enormous number of sightings. Shanti couldn't spot a single bird.

'There goes a grey heron!' Bill cried out, his voice ringing with incredulity at Shanti's dire ineptness. He steered her head along the line of flight the bird had apparently embarked upon. Shanti tried her best but could not locate the large and conspicuous bird. With a frustrated squawk, Bill gave up on her.

'Shanti, look at the horses.' Simon walked over to where she had been left to her own devices.

Shanti focused her binoculars in the direction Simon was pointing but, once again, she could only see pure blue sky. Simon stood behind Shanti and drew her closer to his body, removing the pair of binoculars that had been hopelessly glued to her eyes. He guided her head southwards. There was a pack of thoroughbreds cantering past, a few yards away. They were magnificent, a mass of muscle and energy in motion. Shanti had at last been able to spot some game.

Simon kept his arm around Shanti's shoulders as they followed the others. Bill and the rest seemed to have reached a silent agreement that Shanti was Simon's ken; his partner or, more accurately, his novice charge. They followed behind the others for a while and then broke off from the group and settled down on a mound of soft grass in the morning sun. Simon took out the flask from his rucksack and poured tea into the cap. They shared the tea, passing the cap between them.

'Who knew there were so many birds to watch out for in the city,' Shanti said ruefully as she massaged the muscles on her neck, weary from all the futile craning earlier.

'I'm not much of a birder myself,' Simon confessed. 'It's just nice to come out on these walks once a week or so.'

'What are you doing in this place, anyway?' Shanti asked.

'It's not as bad as you kids make it out to be. You should hear the boys talk about Nairobi. None of you has any patience or the benefit of perspective.'

'We're not kids, you know.' The bird walk and the time spent with Simon suddenly stopped feeling like something grown-ups did.

'You're right, I'm sorry.' Simon looked away so Shanti wouldn't see him smiling. He reached behind and pulled a stick out of the ground. He started to strip the peeling bark off it. 'What am I doing here? Keeping with tradition, I suppose. It's an inevitable stint. I was raised with the expectation that I would perform some sort of service in Africa. My grandfather had been part of the Kenya campaign as an officer in the King's African Rifles. My great-uncle served as governor for East Africa before the Second World War. My father was born in Nairobi and managed a tea estate in Kericho before doing his medical studies in Britain. Then he came back and volunteered at tented field hospitals on the northern border in the eighties.'

'Simon, you're a regular African bwana.' It was Shanti's turn to laugh. 'Just wait till I tell the other *kids* at school!'

Simon shrugged. 'Well, anyway, the family expectation was clear. I too would have to serve time in Africa. For a while I didn't know what I should do. My sister is a relief worker and has worked in Somalia, Rwanda and Zaire. I'm a doctor and have a regular practice in London. But when the pressure became too much—I mean, I either had to get married or do something worthy, according to my dad—I decided to volunteer for six months in a medical camp in Mandera, just across the border with Somalia in northern Kenya.'

'And now what, you're going back to London? You're going to get married?'

'Yes, I think so, probably both, but not straight away. I need a break. And I'm taking care of some things for the family, tying up some loose ends with our investments in the region. Nairobi's a good bridge back to my life in London, emotionally, you know, after being surrounded by all that mayhem at the border. And I need to sort through what I want to do now. I tried working at Nairobi Hospital for a while, but I needed a break from medicine. I like teaching, both the boys and you girls.'

'Breaks from life, investments in Africa. Wairimu says only you mzungus talk this way.'

'Ha! I'm not going to apologize for who I am, especially in this fucking—sorry—in this country.'

'And we're the ones who need the patience and perspective to appreciate where we are! You've ruined that stick, by the way. How are you going to put it back? Typical.'

'Who cares? Not you who can't see anything even with the help of those binoculars that are almost as big as you.' Simon bent and kissed her forehead lightly. A hawk flew swiftly past, cunningly swooping low as it approached its prey—presumably a field mouse or some other small animal. Its huge wings cast a shadow over them. It was the first bird Shanti had managed to see all morning.

She stood and brushed the grass off her clothes. 'I need to get back.'

Simon said nothing and turned away from her as he re-packed his rucksack.

When Shanti returned to the apartment, she could sense Mira and Wairimu waiting for her. Wairimu called out to her from the kitchen but Shanti first went to Mira's room. Wairimu followed her into the bedroom, duster and broom in hand. Shanti sat down by her mother's bed while Wairimu made a great show of dusting the bedroom furniture, refusing to meet Mira's eye. Mira ignored the slight and turned to Shanti.

Shanti could sense the remains of a storm that had swept through the room in her absence and waited in silence until Wairimu had left the room.

'What happened?' she asked Mira. 'Did Lata aunty visit?'

'No,' Mira said. Her face creased into a frown. 'It's Wairimu.'

Wairimu had asked Mira for another loan. Wairimu's sister—the first time Mira had ever heard of this sibling—had died of AIDS, leaving three more children in Wairimu's care. Wairimu had to pay additional school fees, she had also been paying a distant relative in her village to ensure that these children were being fed, clothed, minded. One of the children had fallen sick. She'd first paid the local witch doctor to cure her. It turned out she had malaria and Wairimu had to take her to the local clinic. All these bills had been very costly. She claimed she'd drained her savings.

Mira inquired after Wairimu's sister's husband. 'Couldn't he help with his own children?'

Wairimu had laughed. 'What? That old man? All he does is eat and drink.'

That set Mira off on a tirade about the lack of responsibility African men had towards their families. She seized the newspaper that Carol had left on her bedside table and showed Wairimu an article about the absence of family-planning in Kenya; how Kenyan men refused to partake in birth-control methods; how the increase in births and over-swell of the population was ravaging the economy, not to mention the alarming prevalence of AIDS. Mira declared that it was the responsibility of intelligent African women like Wairimu to teach their men a lesson. The drain on their women's coffers had to stop.

Mira hadn't realized that Wairimu had stopped listening after she had said 'African men'. Wairimu had understood the entirety of Mira's implication. She seethed at the slight against the men of her clan, her race. She turned her back on Mira.

'Oh, ma,' Shanti said to Mira. 'I think we should just give Wairimu whatever she wants. It's too late to change things.'

'It's so easy for you,' Mira told Shanti, her eyes glassy with accusation. 'I've had to live here all my life. You can leave when you're older.'

'What do you want me to do, ma?' Shanti said. 'I'm sorry.'

'You can do whatever you want,' Mira said, looking away. 'I'm tired. I'm tired of all this.'

Shanti left Mira's room. She found Wairimu sitting on the living-room floor next to the ornately carved Lamu chest. Wairimu had opened it and pulled out all their old photo albums. Pictures of a younger Shanti were strewn all around her.

Wairimu looked up at Shanti and smiled. 'Shanti, if you were mine then, so little like that, I would wrap you in a kanga and carry you on my back. And when you wanted to sleep, I would keep you in the front pocket of my apron.'

Shanti put her arms around Wairimu instinctively, unthinkingly, and held her tight, saying they'd pretend that it was true; it would be Shanti's most beloved childhood memory: Wairimu carrying Shanti on her back and rocking her to sleep in her apron. It was how things should have been.

'Acch. You are a silly girl with too many dreams,' Wairimu declared as she shrugged Shanti off her like a lioness would her cub.

Later, before going to sleep, Shanti went to Mira's room to say goodnight. And Mira saw that something different was worrying her daughter. Something bigger than their squabble. Shanti kissed her mother on the cheek, asked Mira if she needed anything. Mira did not know how to answer her. Shanti had brought Mira a glass of milk. She lingered at Mira's bedroom door, looking just like the little girl who used to long to be invited into her mother's bed, to spend the night with her. How careless she had been, Mira thought as she watched her daughter, how casually she had dismissed her, ordering her to return to her own room. It was at moments like these that Mira wished they could be close again, and it pained her. The things Shanti said affected Mira more deeply than if they came from other people. Mira was not going to start a fight with her. Shanti had just come to her, for her, and Mira was not going to waste this precious time they had together. Every time Shanti left her, a small voice inside Mira told her that this could be the last time she would ever see her daughter.

'In our past, I had to make the decision to leave you,' Mira wanted to tell her. 'You were too young to see the danger. You were too young to understand.'

Mira was not asking for what she knew she could never have, for Shanti to forgive her. She was just asking for one clear moment, when they truly understood where they had stood before and where they were now. And she was asking for love. The truest kind that she knew they could still give each other. But the moment, like all the others before, disappeared, and Mira was unable to do anything yet again.

17

FAT CUMULOUS CLOUDS FLOATED in the slate blue of the afternoon sky, their substance seemingly spun from a spool of silvery cotton as they glistened in the bright sun. The reddish-brown of the trees lining the hockey pitch matched the rectangle of earth whose perimeter they skimmed, their extended branches were almost black against the sunlight as they reached for the clement sky.

Neither team had scored yet. The St Joseph's boys were on the other side of the pitch where the ball was, trying to get it through the goal posts. The Kili girls were standing on their own, defending the empty half of the pitch. Mariella had made friends with their team's goalkeeper and, discarding her stick, had sat down at the edge of the pitch, stretching her legs before her to make sure they were in his full view, as she talked to him through his netted enclosure. Suddenly the ball flew towards Shanti. A Sikh boy from the other team was chasing it, the others followed just behind. Shanti couldn't see in the red dust that suddenly enveloped her. She aimed for the area in front of her, hitting the curved edge of her stick hard in the ground. The boy fell over the stick and landed face down on the ground. His turban flew off. The crowd, who was supposed to be cheering for the other side, roared with laughter. Shanti put her hands up in the air, saying she never meant to hit the boy. Simon ran towards her with the coach from the other team, who was waving at the crowd, trying to calm them.

'You did nothing wrong,' Simon shouted to her as he got closer.

Sebu, who had walked up behind Shanti, held her by her shoulders and turned her to face him.

'This, I did not expect from a girl!' he said before covering her mouth with his own. His tongue and teeth were hard as he separated her lips, they hurt Shanti as she received her first kiss.

Simon walked up to them as the cheers from the crowds turned into whistles and hoots.

'This is unacceptable behaviour!' he said, still shouting though he was standing right next to them. His face was red.

'Relax, coach,' Sebu said, patting him on the back before he ran back to the centre of the pitch, waving his hockey stick in the air.

Their team managed to score a goal after that, winning the match against the other school that had lost its morale on its own turf.

When Simon held the door open for them to climb into the combie and drive back to school, he didn't look Shanti in the eye. He got into the passenger seat next to the driver and kept his focus straight ahead.

'We chapaa-ed them, coach!' one of the boys yelled, but Simon didn't turn around.

Shanti could see that the back of his neck was still red and decided not to sit in the seat behind him like she had on the way there. She went to the back of the bus to find Mariella, who was sitting on the goalkeeper's lap.

'And we weren't even at our best; without half the team our strength was only nusu-nusu,' another boy said.

Sebu called Shanti to sit next to him. He positioned himself diagonally, leaning against the window so he could look at his teammates while Shanti sat between his outstretched legs.

'In reality, they weren't that different from us, just more mzungus and muhindis,' someone else said.

While the others talked, Shanti said nothing as she settled back against Sebu's chest. His arms encircled her while he massaged her body. His square fingers worked down her neck, her back, her arms and slowly found their way to the front, moving across the curve of her midriff until they finally came to rest on the dimple beneath her rib cage. Shanti closed her eyes and arched her back against him, allowing herself to enjoy the brief moment.

The conversation drifted on as the team drove back to school. The sun disappeared lazily behind the African tulip trees by the side of the road and Shanti watched in silence as the sky gradually turned from bright blue to orange, then dusky rose into violet.

—

When Shanti got home, she saw Wairimu in the verandah, holding a tray with a cup of tea. Wairimu's eyes were fixed in an accusing stare that choked off Shanti's cheerful greeting. Shanti adopted an expression of casual indifference, hoping Wairimu could not see the places where Sebu had touched her body.

'We won the match,' she said with a smile.

'Tcha!' Wairimu clicked her tongue against her front teeth upbraidingly. 'You need to go to your mother. It is a bad day and you are late. You have made her like this today.'

'Wairimu, it isn't my fault,' Shanti said, surprised at how easily disposed Wairimu was to blame her. 'I'm just a few hours later than usual.'

Wairimu snorted as she turned away from Shanti and walked smartly back indoors.

Mira smiled gratefully when Shanti entered the bedroom. She closed her eyes and pressed her lips against her daughter's forehead.

'Ma, you have to sort out this whole loan thing with Wairimu,' Shanti said straightaway.

'Oh god, you don't know the whole saga.' Mira sighed. There was a story behind this loan request.

Wairimu was treated like a superstar in her family. She earned a substantial constant income and would return to her village, bearing many gifts each time. Her father always slaughtered a goat to celebrate his moneyed daughter's return. Wairimu had left her children in the village under her widowed father's care. She then decided to construct a material sign of success—a concrete home for her family. An ordinary mud hut with a thatched roof would not do. Her house would be made of stone with tin roofing: waterproof, windproof, permanent, a showpiece of urban wealth in her rural village.

Mira had cautioned Wairimu against this, the other villagers would resent her showy display of success. Wairimu took her remarks as a personal belittlement, she felt that Mira did not want her to have a decent house of her own. Mira had looked around her own solid home with all its finery, a house that Wairimu cared for daily, and felt guilt wash over her. So she decided to gift Wairimu the initial instalment for her house.

It was a disaster from the start. Other villagers stole the construction supplies: a sheet of the tin roofing showed up as a table-top in someone's home, the roof of a chicken coop in another, the concrete bricks were used as foundations for fireplace hearths and as rudimentary water-catchment vessels. So Wairimu negotiated her first loan from Mira; she couldn't just leave her house in mid-construction, she reasoned. The house was finally built after her nephews were posted to watch over the supplies day and night.

Then her entire family moved into the stone house. Many more family members than Wairimu had intended—her children, some stray nephews and nieces, her father, and an unexpected addition, his new wife.

Now the new wife was expecting her first baby and wanted every other child out of the house, including Wairimu's children, who had been left under her father's care. Wairimu's father, as the oldest living male member of the household, claimed the property as his customary right, and demanded that Wairimu move her children out of the house. She lost her new home and a shelter for her children.

Mira was furious. She had taken the entire sequence of events extremely personally. There existed a complex bond between Mira and Wairimu. Wairimu, who had been Prashant's housekeeper before he married, had become Mira's first friend in Africa. She had shown the young bride how to take care of her husband's household.

But by its nature, it could not be an equal relationship. Mira would occasionally show interest in the upkeep of her home, discover the silver hadn't been polished or the shelves dusted, and snap at Wairimu.

Wairimu, a woman far beyond her time and circumstance, resented her position in society. She wanted more. The aspiration for a concrete house was just one bead on a long necklace of yearning for material wealth, status, power. When Wairimu and Mira talked about their desires, Wairimu would describe images rich and deep; in her dreams she would see gold glittering in the sun's rays, bountiful rainbows leading to pots full of treasure, all of which she would declare her own.

On a more basic level, Wairimu and Mira were two women managing the same house and running one kitchen. Mira once told Wairimu to put parsley in a dish. Wairimu scoffed, claiming that mint went much better with the recipe. She threw in a handful of the mint she had earlier plucked from the herb garden. With flair and imagination, Wairimu established her domain, her supremacy in the kitchen. Mira fumed and demanded she use parsley in future. She pulled out a cookbook to show Wairimu that it was in fact parsley that was used in this recipe. Wairimu bristled; she could only read when she placed a finger under each letter of every word and tested the sound of the entire combination out loud to herself first.

Throughout the years they had spent together, Mira would confide in Wairimu about her life, her own troubles. Wairimu would comment, comfort and advise her. So Mira felt it was her right to be outraged at Wairimu's situation. She was irate for Wairimu's sake. How dare Wairimu's father throw her children out of the house she herself had built? Why hadn't Wairimu had the sense to establish a landowner's deed for the property? Hadn't Mira told Wairimu the whole stone house initiative was a bad idea?

Even after listening to this story, Shanti told Mira that she had to make an immediate decision to help Wairimu's situation. So, in order to shake out the murky discontentment in their silk curtains, to brush away all those deleterious rumblings under their Afghan carpets, Mira decided to give Wairimu another loan.

18

WAIRIMU AND SHANTI STOOD at the top of the road. Shanti had only a partial view of the gates to their compound through the moonflower trees that lined the pavement. Wairimu was dressed in her Sunday outfit. She was a spiritual leader of her church and was wearing a traditional white cotton dress and matching turban. She spent most Sundays leading her congregation in chanting and dance. This morning, she had decided to skip the service and travel upland to her house in the village instead. She had asked Shanti to accompany her. Shanti felt awkward standing next to Wairimu's pristine figure in her tennis shoes, jeans and sleeveless t-shirt which only accentuated the difference in their existences outside the apartment.

Shanti stared forlornly up the road at the spare metal bars glinting in the pale dawn. Wairimu started to run the beads of her rosary through her fingers, her eyes closed in prayer, as she made up for missing her church service this morning. Shanti fiddled uncomfortably with the beaded leather strap of her kikapu, a dyed sisal bag that she had purchased on impulse at a touristy boutique in the city.

A combie swerved around the corner and stopped in front of them. The driver tooted his horn and a series of musical notes that sounded like an out-of-tune version of the Lambada wafted out of the vehicle. Wairimu hurriedly put the rosary around her neck, tucking the long string of beads and crucifix into the front of her blouse.

'Come, it is our taxi,' she said to Shanti as she walked purposefully to the cantankerous vehicle.

The 'taxi' was in fact a matatu—a private mini-van of the poorest condition, known for cramming in passengers, horrendous driving, illegal drivers and operating without a valid permit. The rust-worn exterior of the small bus had a base coat of white paint and multi-coloured stick figures that looked as if they were participating in a rave party strewn across its sides. The words 'Love Makes the World Go Round' were scrawled across the rear window in bright letters. What appeared to be a bus tout sprang out from the passenger seat and lavishly slid back the van's door before curling into a low bow before Wairimu and Shanti. The tout was a Rastafarian. He wore Ray-Ban style sunglasses, bright yellow shorts, a short-sleeved orange shirt with green parrots on it—unbuttoned in front to display a shiny gold medallion resting against his chest—and a pair of Nike sneakers.

'Habari mama.' He asked Wairimu how she was keeping, presumably in recognition of her religious garb.

'Mzuri tu,' she said, replying that she was just fine.

'Cool baby chica,' slid out of the tout's mouth as he turned to Shanti.

Shanti smiled uncertainly, unsure how she should respond. As she climbed into the van, the tout flashed her a grin, displaying a startlingly white set of teeth against his dark skin and shades.

There were already eight passengers in the matatu. They made space for Wairimu and Shanti in the front row, just behind the driver's seat. Wairimu motioned for Shanti to take the seat by the window. She seized it, immediately sliding the window open and sticking her head out to recover from the stench of sweat and dank air that hit them as soon as they entered the van. Wairimu sat in the middle of the seat, leaving a spot for one more person to sit with them. The tout slammed the door shut and jumped into the seat next to the driver.

Wairimu started speaking to the driver in Kikuyu. Shanti retreated into the van to try and follow the dialogue. The driver turned to regard Wairimu sullenly. His eyes were bloodshot and he chewed continuously on a wad of grass-like substance jammed into the side of his mouth. After she finished speaking, he shrugged and turned back to the steering wheel as he swerved onto the middle of the road.

'What did you say to him?' Shanti asked her.

'Bah, I told him to drive carefully with god in his heart.'

'What is he chewing?'

'Miraa,' said Wairimu with a grimace.

'It's a weed, man,' supplied the tout. 'To keep our driver awake so you can reach your destination alive—with god in your heart.' The driver and he burst into loud guffaws.

The tout turned up the volume of a battered radio which was already blaring African music infused with rap and techno beats. They were most likely over the maximum occupancy limit allowed for this sort of commercial vehicle.

At every corner and roundabout, the driver screeched to a halt to try to pick up potential passengers, beckoning to them via strains of the Lambada. A man and a young boy got in, which made them a total of twelve, or fourteen, including the driver and the tout. The two miraculously fitted in at the back, somewhere behind Wairimu and Shanti. A woman and a baby clambered on and sat beside them. That made it sixteen. A slender youth joined. Seventeen. The tout gave up his seat for a fat woman and a young girl. Nineteen. The van hurtled along, with the tout leaning and waving madly out of the perpetually open door. At least it let in some air. They stopped one more time for a man with a hen tucked under his arm. The man squeezed into the front next to the fat woman. The squawking bird was passed unceremoniously over the passengers' heads to the back window and then shoved on top of the roof. The young girl crawled to the back and sat down. The baby was silently handed over to and unquestioningly taken by the back rows. After the adjustments, shifting and settling—through all of which, Shanti firmly held onto her seat, feeling somewhat comforted with Wairimu on one side of her and an open window on the other—they set out to leave the city. All twenty of them (plus one, including the hen) had managed to fit into the compact, battered vehicle.

They finally reached the fringes of the city. The driver swerved into the shanty towns that covered the small hills on the outskirts of Nairobi. They plundered through thc tangle of mud huts with corrugated tin roofs. The driver seemed to have great fun speeding towards and, at the last second, dodging a medley of goats, chickens, stray dogs and children. The children were in a pitiful condition, they were extremely thin with large stomachs protruding out of their tiny frames. Their clothes were tattered, their hair woolly and matted. Purple scars and bruises marked their faces.

'They are AIDS orphans,' Wairimu said as she watched Shanti stare at them. 'Most of them are children of prostitutes who have died of AIDS.'

'Do they have AIDS too?'

'Some do. Others are just dying because they have no one to look after them.'

'Why isn't the government doing anything for them?'

Wairimu snorted. 'The government? It is men who work in the government and other big jobs that give these prostitutes

AIDS. They need to have too many women to feel important and they refuse to wear condoms.'

'Do you think the new government will do something about it, with its effort to stamp out corruption and all?'

'Please, Shanti. They are all the same, these big men with power. Do you think they care about people like these? Or even people like me? That is why we have to take care of ourselves. We have only god to protect us.'

After delivering her edict, Wairimu remembered her rosary and pulled it out to continue her prayers. Shanti went back to staring out of the window and tried to recover from the desolate image of the shanty towns.

The bus veered onto a tarmac road. Still uncertain whether this was a good thing, since the driver had immediately increased his already high speed and felt free to let go of the steering wheel and use both hands to gesture expressively as he joked with the tout, Shanti continued to focus on the perpetually changing scenery.

They were in maize land. There were nothing but endless fields stretching across the vista. Shanti could see smoke rising in grey tufts at the edge of the horizon.

'All this belongs to your mother's friend, Carol,' Wairimu whispered into Shanti's ear.

'All what?' Shanti said in surprise.

'Carol's father owns the maize factory. This is his land. These Luos pretend they are only interested in academics and look down on our Kikuyu businessmen. But they are big people with big money,' explained Wairimu. 'Weh, weh, weh.' She shook her head and returned to her rosary.

The sun had risen fully over the hills ahead. The bus turned towards it and started to climb to higher ground. The terrain changed. They were now surrounded by sloping hills covered with a patchwork of cultivated greenery. The road became steep. The bus continued at a dangerously high speed, cutting across stretches of hillside. Shanti caught a glimpse of the Great Rift Valley as they rattled past various viewpoints. The driver stopped briefly at one of the viewing areas. Some of the passengers got off, others joined. There were little stalls at the side of the road, displaying rugs, hats and bags made of sheepskin. The stench of untreated skin and hair wafted into the bus as they hurtled onwards once again. The other passengers did not seem to notice the lingering smell of decay. They were jubilant, laughing and talking amongst themselves and occasionally waving to small children who herded goats and sheep by the roadside.

The sky turned iron grey as the van climbed further upland. The air seemed cleaner. Shanti breathed effortlessly. The cultivation on the hillsides had changed as well. They whizzed past coffee farms as they ascended even higher.

The temperature had dropped considerably. They were surrounded by a carpet of emerald green as they drove through tea country. Wairimu tapped Shanti's shoulder and motioned towards something outside. Shanti followed Wairimu's gaze and saw a purple mountain, snow glistening on its peak as it disappeared into the slate sky.

'We are blessed to have seen it today,' Wairimu said in a hushed voice.

'Mount Kenya.'

'Kere-Nyaga,' Wairimu corrected her.

'I learned in school that it's called the Mountain of the Gods.'

'Yes, that is where Ngai—our creator—stays when he visits us.'

'Ngai?' Shanti looked at Wairimu quizzically. 'I thought you were Christian.'

'I am Christian. But I am also Kikuyu. And when I go home I must be Kikuyu first and everything else second.'

The sky darkened and a skein of thunder rolled across it.

'He is moving,' Wairimu whispered.

'Who is moving?' Shanti whispered back.

'Ngai,' Wairimu said reverently as she closed her eyes. 'It sounds like this when he decides to leave his home and go visit some other land.'

Shanti turned towards Wairimu, her curiosity fully awoken, and started to question her about Ngai and the reason for his visits.

'Shh,' Wairimu said to Shanti, her voice still a whisper. 'We must not talk too much about him otherwise he will get angry. And don't look at the sky while he is travelling. It will bring bad luck. We do not know why he visits—sometimes it is for general inspection, at other times he comes bringing blessings or punishment on people.'

They were now surrounded by a grey fog. It started to rain. The van charged up the hillsides. Shanti tried to sneak another look at Mount Kenya but could not see it any more. It had disappeared behind the heavy curtain of cloud.

They turned into the hillside. The tarmac turned to mud. The road, which previously accommodated two lanes of cars, narrowed into a single path. Wairimu asked the driver to stop. Shanti and Wairimu got off and stood on the deep red earth. The tout hung out of the bus and blew Shanti a kiss. She waved at him cheerily, feeling more optimistic now that she was safely on solid ground. The matatu lumbered away, leaving large spatterings of red mud in its wake.

They walked through a township covered in a shift of mist. There were small stores in tin shacks, displaying brightly dyed cloths with ruddy patterns, gas lamps and little coal stoves. Shanti bought a kanga and wrapped it around herself like a shawl. They passed more shacks which housed a bar, a barber's shop, additional dukas. There was a petrol station at the end of the township.

It was almost noon when they reached Wairimu's village. The strong sun was muted by an insipid layer of fog that lingered over them. The huts in Wairimu's village had a wooden frame, the walls were made of mud, the roofs out of thatch. The concrete house that Wairimu had built from scratch loomed larger and taller than the rest. Each home had a shamba, where sukuma wiki and carrots were grown. A subdivision at one end was cultivated with maize and other staples, the remaining unused land was home to roaming goats and chickens. Thin blue smoke rose from the houses, presumably from jikos. The carbon from the lighted coal stoves made Shanti's eyes sting. There was a shout of delight as someone recognized Wairimu. A few women came running out of their houses to embrace her, while the men stood at the edges, watching and smiling. Wairimu started foraging in her bag and produced a motley assortment of gifts from the city—some of which, Shanti noticed, were from their apartment—battery-operated flashlights, knitting needles, wool, balls of string. It was evident that Wairimu was regarded as an elder and provider for her community.

She pulled Shanti forward to introduce her, speaking in Kikuyu. Some of the younger girls rushed back into their houses. They returned wearing shoes and with their heads covered in scarves. Wairimu proudly led Shanti through the village, towards her house. The young girls followed in clumps of twos and threes, nudging each other and giggling as they whispered and pointed at her. As Shanti was about to enter Wairimu's home, one girl rushed up to her and said something shyly in Kikuyu as she pointed at Shanti's bag. Shanti turned to Wairimu for an explanation.

'She wants you to take a picture of her and her friends,' said Wairimu, not sounding at all approving.

Shanti explained that she did not have a camera. Wairimu translated for her.

'Tell them I apologize for not bringing one,' she told Wairimu.

'Bah,' Wairimu replied. 'They should be more interested in helping their mothers than dressing up so you can take pictures of them.'

She gave them what sounded like a serious telling off in Kikuyu and they scattered immediately.

Wairimu stared straight ahead as they walked past the house that she'd built and lost. A young woman stepped out onto a concrete platform—the only porch in the village—and began to sweep, causing the dust to rise all around her. Shanti kept her head down, avoiding the subject of the house and the person who'd emerged from it, even though they were the most remarkable subjects in the village. Wairimu tucked her arm into Shanti's and swept her inside her new home, which was only a few huts away.

The main room in Wairimu's home was modestly decorated. There was a wooden table against the wall, a battery-operated radio in the opposite corner. Shanti recognized the mosaic she and Mira had made for Wairimu years ago with Mira's broken tea set placed decoratively in the middle of the table. There was a knitted blanket, which Mira had given Wairimu then as well, spread out on the stone floor in front of a cot. Wairimu led Shanti through the room to a small courtyard on the other side. An old man was sitting by a lit jiko. They walked up to him. Wairimu bowed in front of him and placed her hands in his. The old man was Wairimu's older brother. He did not speak English and Wairimu had to interpret for Shanti.

A young woman came out into the courtyard carrying mugs

of sweet milky tea and fried bread. Shanti recognized her from the pictures of her son and his bride which Wairimu kept in her quarters. Wairimu's daughter-in-law also brought out low stools and they sat around the small jiko to warm themselves. Wairimu's son was away, working in a nearby town. A neighbour, a woman of about Wairimu's age, came over with a dish of food. It was some sort of roasted root, perhaps cassava or yam. The woman handed the dish to Wairimu's daughter-in-law and joined them.

Shanti sat silently while the others talked in Kikuyu, exchanging news. Lunch was brought out, a meal consisting of chapatis made of white flour, chicken in a soupy liquid, cassava, and fruit to follow. Wairimu's daughter-in-law said something in a grumbling tone punctuated with disapproving clicks of her tongue as she served them.

'She is complaining that I never warn her about my visits. She is angry this time because I have brought you with me and she did not prepare anything special. But if I told her I was coming, and with a guest, she would have prepared a feast with every goat and chicken we own, and then asked me to send her money from Nairobi to replace the slaughtered animals.' Wairimu laughed and slapped her thighs.

Shanti asked Wairimu to tell her daughter-in-law that the food was sufficient and delicious. The woman bowed in front of Shanti while the others nodded.

Then the old man said something to Wairimu and pointed at Shanti. When Shanti turned to her for a translation, Wairimu looked at her, her eyes piercing.

'He wants me to tell you that he is praying for the long-awaited celebration of the death of your mother.'

Shanti gasped. Wairimu patted her back as she tried to recover from this comment. The old man's voice became agitated as he talked to Wairimu. She replied in a soothing voice and then turned to Shanti again.

'The Kikuyu do not fear death, Shanti,' she explained. 'In fact, we think it is a blessing to have someone you love die. That way they can always be with you. Their spirit will guide and protect you.'

Shanti nodded vigorously and smiled weakly at the old man, trying to assure him that his words had not offended her.

The old man picked up a handful of the red mud that made up the earth here and said something to Shanti.

'He wants you to know that the soil, it provides a shelter for the spirits of the dead forever,' Wairimu translated.

Shanti nodded and looked down at the plate of food on her lap, blinking away her tears, hoping that no one had noticed them.

Wairimu's neighbour said something.

Wairimu smiled and said to Shanti, 'She is saying I should tell you the story of Mukuru Muriati's niece. This is the story: there is a young girl whose mother and father tell her to go to her uncle's house because they are dying. On her way there, an ogre stops her to ask where she is going. The ogre then goes to the uncle's house and pretends to be the niece. The uncle believes the ogre and takes it into his house. When the niece comes, he treats her very badly and does not allow her into his home. Her now dead parents watch how the child is being mistreated. The girl sings a song to her dead parents about her bad treatment and when the uncle hears the song he understands his mistake. He kills the ogre and takes the girl into his house. So through death, her parents were able to keep an eye on the girl and make sure she was safe.'

The neighbour started to sing. The others laughed and clapped their hands in rhythm. Wairimu sang part of the song in English for Shanti's benefit.

My father's spirits do ask: Daughter of your father,
  where do you sleep?
On the ashes by the fireside.
My mother's spirits do ask: Daughter of your mother,
  where do you eat from?
From a broken calabash.

Shanti joined in the clapping and laughter to show that she was no longer upset and later thanked the old man for his blessing.

After the meal, Wairimu took Shanti for a walk through her shamba. There was an old windmill in the distance. Shanti asked her if the villagers used it.

'No,' she replied. 'The Norwegians came and built it a long time ago, but it has never worked. Come, I'll show you where we get our water.'

They walked back to the house and Wairimu pointed to an open pipe that ran along one side of the tin roof. The end of the pipe dropped into a rusty metal barrel set at the side of the house. It was a rudimentary method of collecting rainwater.

'What do you do during the dry season?' Shanti asked.

'There is a bore hole we can walk to, or we buy cans of water from the town.'

They continued their walk in the shamba. The afternoon was cold and damp; the raw wind cut into their skin. Shanti wrapped the kanga tighter around her. The lush plantations of tea and coffee that they had driven through to get here seemed a world away, the bright lights of Nairobi even further.

When they returned to the house, their car was parked in front of it. Shanti could see Samuel in the driver's seat.

'I am staying here for the night so I asked Samuel to pick you up,' Wairimu said.

Shanti hugged Wairimu. She thanked her housekeeper for inviting her to her home.

Wairimu waved her aside. 'Shanti, you are like my own child and it makes me happy to bring you here. But now I know you need to go home.'

Shanti felt her spirits lift as she sank into the warmth of the car as they bumped towards the tarmac road.

Darkness fell as they sped easily down the hills and back towards the city. Shanti could see the burnished glow of lights in the distance, looming larger with every kilometre they traversed, and dreamt of the familiar warmth of her home.

There was chaos in the compound. The grounds had been left unguarded for one evening and there was a break-in. A message had been dispatched, a smoke signal sent, that there lay open an unmanned habitation that night, ripe for a raid.

Several cars were wrecked: a Range Rover was stolen; a BMW had its side-view mirrors stripped, hubcaps purloined and tyres slashed. Car radios had been ripped out, car batteries had vanished. Only one apartment was broken into: it stood out, orphaned in darkness, the phone line cut, the windows broken, as the residents around woke up to screaming wails of car alarms in the middle of the night. Fearful that their own lives might be splintered next, the tenants retreated into their homes. They watched and waited for the storm to pass, the dust to settle.

Shanti walked into the apartment on her own, wishing she hadn't let Samuel drop her off outside the gate. She'd felt guilty that Wairimu had asked him to come on his day off. Everything seemed broken. The handle on the front door, the two locks and chains that should have prevented an unwelcome entrant, the lamp and shade in the hallway, the portrait of Prashant. The frame hung crookedly, the glass was fractured, splinters lay on the ground among scattered petals and the smashed diya. The broken mess had been trodden upon. Shanti could make out prints of safari boots across the floor. Shanti found Mira in bed. The bedclothes completely covered her body so Shanti couldn't see any part of her. Shanti pulled the razai back from the top of Mira's head, frightened of what she might find underneath. There was blood. It had tangled Mira's thin hair into damp, shiny clumps. Some of it had travelled in uneven lines along one side of Mira's face, collecting in the crevices, in the hollows around her closed eye, under her nostril, in the indentations of her ear.

'Ma,' Shanti whispered. She touched Mira's forehead.

'Have they gone?' Mira asked, her eyes still shut.

'Yes. What happened? What did they do?'

'They hit me. I was cut by the blade of the panga.'

'Ma, I'll go get help.' Shanti tried not to cry. She was afraid of her tears spilling onto Mira and causing her more pain.

'No.' Mira held onto Shanti's wrist. 'Don't leave me alone here.'

Shanti brought a basin of hot water and a towel from the bathroom. She started sponging the side of Mira's head. The continual scrape of the towel against Mira's skin as Shanti swabbed the places marked by blood, broken in pauses when she soaked the towel in the bowl of water, was hypnotic. The rhythmic movement filled the silent apartment. The water had turned a dull red by the time Shanti finished.

'Ma, this cut is too deep. I think you need stitches. Please, let me go get help.'

'Okay,' Mira said. She closed her eyes. Shanti didn't know if she was dropping off to sleep or out of consciousness.

'Ma, try to stay awake. Please. I'll be back in less than ten minutes.' Shanti shook Mira, forcing her to keep her eyes open.

Shanti ran out of the apartment and across the courtyard to the other building. She ran up the four flights of stairs to Carol's apartment. When no one answered the doorbell, she knocked on the door. There was no one at home. She rushed back to her own building and ran up two floors to Flip's apartment. She started shouting for Flip before she reached the door. She banged on the door and then tried the handle and found it unlocked. Flip wasn't there. Shanti tried her phone and found it was working. She called Lata. Lata told Shanti she would come at once to take Mira to the doctor. Shanti asked her if they should call the police. Lata told her to do nothing and talk to no one else until she arrived.

No one ever informed the authorities of these crimes against their homes. At the grassroots, the keepers of order were most often involved in the crimes themselves. Residents shied away from inviting policemen into their homes after a crime for fear that the visit might turn out to be a pretext, an excuse to survey the locale in order to accomplish a subsequent, better-planned raid. Meanwhile, the higher authorities, the politicians, lived in a vacuum cushioned against these events. They looked away and talked away the disorder around them, for to admit to any of the carnage would be to admit to their own complicity; admit that the position and comfort they enjoyed were part of the pillage instead of payment for the services they provided to the state.

Shanti lay next to Mira on the bed, willing the warmth of her own body to seep into her mother's. Mira's head rested against Shanti's breast. Shanti stroked her mother's hair slowly, avoiding the place where she'd been cut. The wound still looked raw but the bleeding had stopped. Mira's eyes were bright, feverish even.

'Shanti, you must listen to me.'

'Ma, not now, you're tired. So am I.'

'No, Shanti. You have to listen. You need to.'

'Ma, please, let's just rest. Lata aunty's on her way so we can take you to the doctor. We'll see what they've taken tomorrow.'

Mira pressed on, 'It's time, Shanti. Hear me now. I don't know if I'll be able to tell you properly ever again.' Her voice broke into a sob and she looked away.

Shanti stroked away the thin strands of hair from her mother's forehead, softly blowing on the top of her head with the hope that it would soothe her. 'Ma, ma.'

As the night deepened into an endless void of darkness, Shanti moved to the foot of the bed and sat directly opposite Mira. She stared at her mother's drawn face, the skin stretched across her thin bones. Shanti felt as if she had known this would happen all along. The memory, the solidity of it, streamed through her. The night clouded her vision like a spool of cotton, muffling her ability to peer into the flickering shadows and see past them to the truth of their sequestered time.

Mira looked up. 'Let me tell you about Sita,' she whispered.

Shanti had not sought after Sita but for a few scarce dreams these past months. But that was where her mother forced her to go now, and there was nothing that could shield her against it.

'You have to know about Shakuntala and Sita,' Mira begged.

Shanti looked into Mira's eyes and saw an image that she knew intimately. She saw a reflection that was her own.

PART FOUR

India

19

SHAKUNTALA'S DAY BEGAN AT the household shrine where each woman in the family made a quick offering to the gods. Her mornings were spent fetching water, cooking and looking after her young daughter, Sita. In the afternoon she worked with the men in the fields. Shakuntala lived in the obscurity of the desert, in a village that was several miles away from any source of water.

In the marriage market of Rajasthan, an area riddled with drought, a potential groom's worth was assessed not by the money he had or the land he owned but by the distance of his home from the nearest body of water. The drought in Rajasthan had cruelly lessened the burden of raising a daughter. It allowed Shakuntala's parents to reduce an extravagant dowry demand from her future in-laws because Shakuntala was married to a man who lived in a village that did not have its own well. The girls that were married into families living in this village led a life of physical hardship and few families were at ease when they sent their daughters here.

After the wedding, Shakuntala's husband, Ravi, bought a truck and a few camel carts to fetch water from a source village where water was stored and supplied to other villages, which made life a little easier for them. But even then, the source village only got water once a month, from tankers commissioned by the British rulers.

If Shakuntala's parents could have afforded a decent dowry for her, the possibility of a marriage to Ravi wouldn't have even been considered. He presented a dismal future for any prospective bride: not only did he come from a remote village with no independent means of water supply, he was also the sole provider for his family, a family that consisted of his older brother, Rakesh, who was a widower and refused to work; two unmarried sisters, Sareeta and Padma, with no chance of ever becoming brides since there were no dowries set aside for their marriages, though Padma, the younger of the two, still held out hope of being given away; and his half-witted brother, Pramod, who was widely regarded as the village idiot.

After her morning prayers, Shakuntala picked up the empty pitcher, careful not to place it on her head. She had unwittingly committed that crime when she was pregnant with Sita: she had balanced the empty earthen vessel on top of her head and was crossing the courtyard outside her mud hut on her way to the village when Sareeta, her older sister-in-law, spied her.

'Wretched girl,' Sareeta had shouted as she struck Shakuntala across her face. The clay pitcher fell on the dry earth and smashed into a million pieces. 'Have you no sense? You have angered the water gods and now a bad omen will fall on our household.'

'A bad omen?' Shakuntala cried out indignantly, for she was only seventeen and still hadn't learned that life would fare better for her if she kept her mouth shut. 'How can I bring any more ill-fortune to this miserable house?'

'Now you will surely bring a daughter into this house, you ungrateful hussy,' Sareeta said, her eyes glittering triumphantly. 'Just wait till I tell my brother what you've done and then see what he does to you.'

That evening when Ravi staggered home after his usual bout of heavy drinking, he was met by Sareeta and Pramod in the middle of the courtyard. As Ravi listened to Sareeta's agitated complaints, Pramod started jumping around them like an excited monkey.

Pramod followed Ravi as he strode into his quarters. He clapped his hands as he watched his brother beat Shakuntala.

'You foolish woman!' Ravi yelled as he kicked her into a corner of her small room. 'Of what use are you if you don't bear me sons?'

Shakuntala lay whimpering on the earthen floor while Ravi stumbled into his adjoining room and fell head first on the charpoi, the only rope bed in the house. They stayed this way every night until Sita was born and for most nights afterwards, unless Ravi fell on Shakuntala in a drunken mess, wriggling and squirming on top of her during his occasional futile attempts to produce a boy.

Before Shakuntala embarked on her daily search for water to bathe herself and her child, she went to check on Sita. The water Ravi brought home was severely rationed. It was mainly used for cooking and for Ravi and his siblings. There was never any amount allocated for Shakuntala's personal use.

They didn't even allow Shakuntala to use any water during Sita's birth. Shakuntala had lain on the bare floor of her mud hut while the village midwife wordlessly cut the umbilical cord and placed the baby on Shakuntala's abdomen. The old woman then left in a hurry, knowing she would not be praised for delivering a daughter into the household.

Shakuntala had called out to her sisters-in-law for water to wash herself and her newborn child but her cries went unheeded. They continued with their day as usual; they wanted no part in easing the arrival of another girl into this house. Their silence would teach the girl a lesson and show Shakuntala her true place in their household.

Hours later, Shakuntala, still faint from the delivery, dragged herself and her baby out of the hut and into the courtyard. There, under the heat of the desert sun, Shakuntala rubbed herself and the child down with sand. It was there, as she scraped off the blood and mucus covering her baby, that she decided she would name the child Sita, daughter of the earth. For surely, Shakuntala thought, the earth would prove to be a better mother to the baby girl than Shakuntala could ever be in her ill-fated existence in this bitter house.

Sita, now four years old, lay curled up in one corner of the earthen floor, fast asleep. Shrugging off the memories of her daughter's birth, Shakuntala took her chunni and wrapped it around her daughter. She lifted the sleeping child onto her lap and tied the ends into a knot at her shoulder. Then she walked across the courtyard and towards the village, the empty earthen pot resting on one hip, her child slung across the other.

Across the courtyard, Pramod leaned against the gatepost, muttering to himself.

'Oye,' he yelled out to her.

Shakuntala walked past him, seeing through him as he tried to lunge at her. She had learned to ignore his presence.

'Bhabhi, haven't you heard?' he spluttered, saliva streaming like milk out of the side of his mouth. 'Ravi bhaiyya is no more.'

Shakuntala stopped as if struck motionless by a stroke of lightning. She turned and stared into his bulging eyes.

'What did you just say?' she demanded.

'He didn't come home last night, or didn't you notice?'

Pramod said. 'He's dead. His truck was in an accident on the bus route and they're arranging to bring back his body.'

Shakuntala's knees buckled under her for a second and as she tried to steady herself the pot slipped from her grip. It hit the ground and splintered into several pieces.

'Oh no, now you've done it. You've really gone and ruined things,' Pramod yelped, clutching his head in his hands.

'Shut up, you fool,' Shakuntala said furiously as she bent down to pick up the shards of broken clay.

As they waited for the arrival of their brother's body, the two older siblings plotted and planned, congratulating each other on their good fortune—no, even more so, on their cunning, the infinite depths of their connivance. Shakuntala, they ordained, would have to commit sati. By being burnt alive, she would commit a blessed act of self-sacrifice, of complete sublimation. They would erect a shrine in her name, call her Sati Mata, and every Hindu woman would envy her position as the pure mother. And they would be rid of another mouth to feed, one that was never really their own.

Rumours that the re-enactment of the spectacle of sati—a custom that had been outlawed in India in the early nineteenth century but remained a hidden practice—spread as fast as a desert wind across the sparse expanse of the region.

While they waited for Ravi's corpse to return to the household, the older siblings chose the site for the ceremony. Why, it made perfect sense to keep the sati sthal in the very spot where Shakuntala had cared for her husband. They would burn her right outside the house. In the middle of the courtyard, in front of the mud hut with the thatched roof, Shakuntala would die voluntarily, painlessly and without protest, fortified by the forces of religious belief.

The toxic desires of brother and sister raced through the surrounding villages by way of the women who gathered to collect water at the village wells and the bus drivers who manoeuvered the desert routes, pausing at the tea stalls that marked the periphery of the villages along the way. News spread of the imminent wonder, the girl who would burn herself for her husband and bring salvation to everyone in the region.

In a mere few days, a brother and a sister, scheming in their home deep inside the kernel of the Thar Desert, had created a new goddess.

Shakuntala didn't know of the events that had occurred the morning Pramod had told her about her husband's death. Rakesh and Sareeta had rushed back to the house, bursting with uncharacteristic vigour. They had assumed especially busy and self-important airs as they hustled Shakuntala into her room and dragged in Ravi's charpoi for her to sleep on. They fussed over her, giving her warm milk sweetened with crushed almonds to drink. Shakuntala had fallen asleep immediately. She woke up periodically, not sure if it were day or night, only to be fed more of the delicious milk and fall asleep again, smiling in her dreams as she counted her blessings, for she was being treated with such extravagant indulgences.

'Ma, wake up. Come on, get up.' Sita tugged at her slumbering mother. 'What's the matter with you, ma?'

Shakuntala forced open her eyelids, they felt as heavy as iron. She staggered to her feet and lurched out of the hut. The sun blinded her as she looked out onto the courtyard. She rubbed her eyes, blinking rapidly several times, not believing what she saw. Yet the image remained. Across the courtyard and beyond the gate was a field of bodies, swaying coconuts above their heads. Cold fear uncoiled within her, jolting her wide awake as she processed the chanting that streamed towards her: Sati Mata ki jai. Sati ki pati ki jai.

Shakuntala retreated into the shadows of the mud house with Sita tugging at her sari.

As the wave of spectators advanced into their village, local businesses thrived. Provisional shacks were set up overnight by the sides of the roads for the crowds as they entered the village and made their way to the sati sthal. The village centre had turned into a fête. Food, coconuts, flowers and incense were being sold. Artists painted gaudy pictures of the anticipated event. Using traditional dyes derived from iron, indigo, jasmine, pistachio and saffron, they drew figures of a virtuous bride sitting upright on the pyre, smiling beatifically with her dead husband laid out before her. Orange flames surrounded them. In the bright blue sky above, Shiva threw his shaft of omniscient light upon the woman.

Ravi's family took a cut from every vendor, artist and entrepreneur. They had been told that more people were on their way to the sati sthal. Brother and sister laid out a plan to keep the crowds pouring in. First, there would be the sati ceremony, the actual burning of the bride. Then there would be another ceremony in the village on the thirteenth day after Shakuntala's immolation—they would hold a chunari mahotsav for all those worshippers who couldn't make it in time for the sati ceremony. On that day they would place Shakuntala's bridal veil on the pyre as a final tribute. Rumour had it that the chunari would ascend and vanish into the sky in front of everyone.

Thousands of villagers would come to behold such a wonder. But why stop there? A temple would bring worshippers for an eternity. They would claim that any affliction could be cured by the Maha Sati, provided one had true belief. Shakuntala's act, they would tell everyone, had made her divine and her devotees would have their prayers answered when they visited the temple. The rumour took on a life of its own. Strangers described in detail the powers and benefits of the sati who would be purified of all corruption and attain perfection, moksha, a divine silence of the gods. The promise of endless cures, miracles and marvels burgeoned throughout the desert and Ravi's family started acquiring donations to erect a temple over the sati sthal.

It was here, in the dark recesses of the mud hut, that Shakuntala found brother and sister squatting on low stools, hunched over piles of coins.

'Oh, look who's finally woken up,' Sareeta said as she stretched.

'Just in time. Ravi's body is arriving this afternoon,' said Rakesh.

'I won't do it!'

Shakuntala's in-laws stood up, towering over her.

'Ungrateful woman, look at what we're doing for you. You will be worshipped by all as the pinnacle of womanhood. We've immortalized you, made you the dedicated wife, the beloved mother of sons, sacrificing through eternities. None of which you remotely came close to in your life.'

'I will not die at your will. You'll have to take me kicking and screaming to the pyre and everyone will see that you have forced me into it.'

'Shut up, you idiot. What future do you have ahead of you, anyway? A social outcast never to be seen in public, a widow,' Sareeta said.

'My parents would kill you if they found out,' Shakuntala said, trembling.

Rakesh laughed. 'Your parents—who sold you into this marriage? Do you think they care about you? They'll celebrate your death and thank us for giving them a place in history. They'll be the parents of a new goddess, the most revered Sati Mata of our time.'

Shakuntala shrank back into her room, defenceless against the cavernous truth her in-laws had spoken. She had no choice.

As the truck bringing Ravi's body rolled into the small village, raising masses of believers behind it as it headed towards her house, Shakuntala reached for the milk laced with sweet opium and fell into deep unconsciousness. The night before her sati ceremony, Shakuntala dreamt of being burnt.

Surrounded by chanting throngs of fevered believers, Shakuntala was stumbling towards the funeral pyre. Sareeta and Padma were distributing flowers and fruit to the other women present who were fortunate enough to be married. As bare-chested Rajput boys holding swords circled the unlit pyre, the sisters-in-law pried open Shakuntala's mouth and placed a pearl in it, bidding her to pray to Agni for a blessed entry into the flames. The surging crowds recited mantras. They threw handfuls of ghee on top of the wood.

Shakuntala recoiled at the sight of the pile of wood, but Rakesh took hold of her and tied down her hands and feet as they buried her under the firewood. He secured the knots and tested the load to make sure she could not escape. Pramod was bid to light the fire. As the flames licked Shakuntala's flesh, she struggled to get away from the funeral pile but was prodded into submission by the wheeling youths and their long thin swords. The fire died out for a moment and Shakuntala, who was partially burnt, pleaded for compassion. The fire was re-lit by Rakesh, aided this time by Sareeta, who made sure it wouldn't be extinguished once again, and Shakuntala was burnt alive.

Shakuntala woke up, drenched in sweat. Her head pulsed in starbursts of sharp pain. Padma was shaking her and speaking rapidly, quicker and keener than she ever had in her entire life. She had offered to give Shakuntala the night's dose of milk and hadn't put opium in it. She told Shakuntala she had to escape that night. She could walk, run, hitch rides to the city. She had heard they had factories there, shops where they paid women money for their bandhni work.

Like every other village woman, Shakuntala knew the skill of tying knots and dying material, binding and rebinding pinhead wisps of cloth to create complex patterns of dots, circles, squares and stripes. Or she could work as a cook, cleaner or sweeper in one of the stone houses there. Shakuntala could do anything, as long as she could escape the death contrived for the following morning.

But what of Sita? Shakuntala could not think of any means to help her daughter. Either way, Sita would be left without her. Shakuntala knew she was of no use to the girl in any case. Sita would have to live out her own life, be another puppet in the hands of fate. At least she would have Padma to look out for her. Padma, frightened of being caught helping Shakuntala, slipped back to her room before anyone woke up, leaving Shakuntala alone now that she was fully alert.

Shakuntala crawled out of the charpoi and onto the mud floor. She crouched low and began to dress. She packed nothing, desiring no memories of her life here. She moved quietly to the entrance of the house. She could hear the others snore as she padded silently past them. Shakuntala stopped for a moment and quickly returned to her room. There, she pulled out the chunari that Sareeta had kept in a basket in preparation for the ceremony. She tore at it, ripping the bright red material with its gaudy zardozi embroidery to shreds.

The courtyard was quiet. The sky was clear, frighteningly open for all the gods to observe Shakuntala commit her crime. Her silhouette as she slid across the courtyard threw divergent shadows on the ground. Shakuntala felt as if an army was following her, tracking her every move. The gate was bolted. She could see rows of coconuts and bodies stretched across the narrow winding lanes of the village. They slept there, waiting to participate in her murder at the first light of day. She could not escape through the village. She was trapped. Shakuntala turned back and rushed through the courtyard to the house. She stopped at the entrance and flattened herself against the mud wall. She clutched her way around the side of the house, passing by the slumbering bodies of her in-laws. At the back of the hut, Shakuntala got down on all fours. She crawled through the vegetable patch, wriggling on her stomach under the bushes of chillies. Finally, she reached the boundary wall surrounding the village. As she prepared to hoist herself over it, something grabbed her left leg. It was Sita.

'Take me with you,' her daughter whispered.

'No, Sita.' Shakuntala's voice was harsh, urgent. 'Go back to the house and sleep.'

'No.' Sita was obstinate. 'You're not going anywhere without me.'

Shakuntala looked around desperately. Clouds had begun to gather in the sky. The heavens rumbled, heavy with threat. Shakuntala lifted her daughter to her hip. They both tumbled over the wall and fell into the fields.

Shakuntala ran with Sita clutching her. Her daughter gripped her body with every one of her fingers and toes. Shakuntala could see only a few paces ahead of her. The air was suddenly thick with dust. She ran madly, blindly, through the fields of millet and maize. She could hear angry roars behind her, above her. She could not make out if they originated from man or god.

As Shakuntala neared the edge of the cultivation, all she could see was sand. It raged around her like fury. The howling wind strangled the cries of fear inside her, inside Sita. The figures were honing in towards them. Shakuntala turned and saw their outlines in the cascades of dust. A sharp object struck the middle of her back. She could feel hot puddles of blood bubble out of her skin and trickle down her legs. Another object hit her on the side, winding her. Her arms around Sita were wrenched away as she breathed in a mouthful of grit. She could feel her daughter whimper as her tiny body dangled at her side. Sita's grip around her mother's neck was cast in iron as she swung against Shakuntala's body.

Mother and daughter ran into the sea of desert in that state, their eyes squinting, their teeth bared. The red rain of sand and dust covered them as they surged forward. Shakuntala felt dizzy. She could see nothing but blood. She was defeated as the storm raged around her. She realized that Sita's only chance of survival was if she separated her from herself. She could, at least, do something to shape her daughter's future. She tore Sita off herself and lay her on the earth. Let her daughter assume her own existence, wrought by her namesake, the goddess who was born of the earth and discovered by a king while ploughing the ground in preparation for a sacrifice. By leaving Sita, Shakuntala was giving her daughter a new incarnation, the possibility of life. She started to run, diverting the crowd away from Sita. As the storm closed in, Shakuntala could hear the whisper of her daughter's heartbeat against her own skin, feel the sigh of her breath against her neck. Shakuntala stood still. She turned around to face the onslaught as it swept over her.

After the storm broke, brittle splinters of light poked through the clouds separating in the sky. A breeze settled on Sita's shoulders like a fine skein as she rose from the ground. The wet moving desert beneath her feet erased her footprints. When the villagers tried tracking them, no trace remained.

PART FIVE

Kenya

20

LATA ARRIVED HALF AN hour after Shanti had called her. An ambulance followed her car. They put Mira on a stretcher. Lata didn't let Shanti climb into the back of the ambulance with Mira. She got in herself and ordered Shanti to go to her house with her driver and wait for her there. After the ambulance left, Shanti told Lata's driver to leave, she refused to sit in the car and go to the Patels' home.

Shanti returned to the apartment and went to her room. They had left it untouched. They'd known where to go, what to take. They'd stolen artifacts from the living room, the carpet and curtains from the dining room, the little jewellery and money Mira had in her bedroom. Things barely worth the trouble of a break-in. The Sharmas didn't have as much as the other, untouched apartments.

Shanti slipped out of the apartment through the back door. She flickered silently across the stone path towards the parking lot. She was stiff as a pole, rigid with the shock of the events of the evening, of seeing her mother in that state, of listening to her mother's story, the story of Sita and Shakuntala. She slid into their car and adjusted the rearview mirror and seat. She felt hollow, like a skeletal shell trying to manoeuvre a machine meant to be operated by whole human beings.

It was very misty. Some of the clouds that blocked the sky earlier in the night had descended to the ground. Shanti was not used to pressing the pedals and lurched onto the street in fits and starts. The mist swirled around her in ribbons and rags. The streetlights were dimmed and stood far apart from each other on the empty roads.

She made her way to Nairobi Hospital. She followed the lights of the ambulance still flashing outside the emergency room. She couldn't find her mother or Lata. Finally, someone sent her to another wing. They'd already put Mira into a room.

Mira's room was jam-packed, crammed full with vials and injections, the apparatus of the drips, a hospital trolley and stands, plastic tubes and bags. Mira was sleeping. The hospital was strict, visitors could not stay in the room with the patient. Lata had already left. Shanti sat in the waiting room and checked on her mother after an hour. A nurse was in the room, watching over Mira, monitoring the drips, administering medicine. She told Shanti to go home and return the next day when Mira would be awake and the doctor would be available to talk to her.

Shanti went to the car. She threw away the ticket she'd received for parking behind the ambulance outside the ER. She reversed in stuttered movements, unable to coordinate the clutch, brake and accelerator properly. It was still dark. The spare light of the street lamps threw eerie shadows across the city. The clouds were mobile, moving rapidly through the indigo-black expanse, baring and concealing the stark moon and stars sprinkled in the sky. Shanti drove through the city in this translucent dark. The headlights of the car suddenly revealed and silhouetted trees, buildings and other obscure objects that hung over her from the edges of the road.

A figure loomed out of the shadows into the middle of the street. It was a woman in tattered clothes, stumbling across the road. Shanti quickly swerved as the woman flailed, her arms stretching into the beam of the headlights. Shanti drove past the gates to their apartment. She staggered down the bumpy road towards Simon's bungalow, finally stopping a little too close to the gate. The askari, abruptly woken from his slumber by the flashing headlights, warily shone his torch into the car. After he had ascertained that she posed no potential hazard to the vicinity under his watch, the guard let Shanti into the grounds. She left the car in the middle of the driveway and ran up the steps to the front door. The askari watched her curiously as she rattled the gong that hung on the heavy wooden door.

'Shanti, what on earth are you doing here?' Simon mumbled as he unhinged the chain and turned the padlock.

'I'm so sorry, I've woken you. I shouldn't have come,' she stammered.

'No, no, I was just reading over this—thing.' Simon slid his palms over his eyes, trying to get them to focus.

He had clearly been asleep. He was wearing only pyjama bottoms, his hair was rumpled and he had a diffused look about him as he stood in the doorway, squinting at her. Then consciousness shifted into him and he stared at Shanti, now alert.

'Shanti, you're shivering. Come inside.'

Shanti went in and sat by a wood stove on a low carved cot covered with large patchwork cushions. There was a brightly coloured wool rug on the floor and an old Zanzibari chest in the middle of the room that served as a coffee table.

Shanti followed the smell of the coffee brewing in the kitchen. Simon had put on a light cotton sweater over his pyjama bottoms. He looked less scruffy, more awake, his hair was patted down after he'd hurriedly splashed water over his face and head. He poured the coffee into two mugs and topped it off with brandy.

'Here, drink this. You'll feel better.' He placed a mug in her hands.

'I almost ran over someone,' Shanti said weakly.

'Where?'

'A woman came out of nowhere at me on the road on my way here.'

'You didn't stop, did you?' he asked, his voice sharp.

Shanti shook her head.

'Good girl,' he replied in a calmer manner.

'I felt bad, she looked like she needed help,' Shanti said.

'She was most likely part of a pack of thieves, or if she had been attacked, her assailants could have been close by. There's nothing you can do about these things.'

Shanti sipped the laced coffee silently, letting the gritty liquid warm her. Simon reached over and smoothed back the strands of hair that had fallen over her face.

'These memories I have, you know…' Shanti hesitated. 'My mother, it's not her fault. They came. She's destroyed. I have nothing.'

'Shh,' Simon whispered, brushing away the tears on her cheeks. 'It'll be all right.'

In the still, soundless warmth of his house, Shanti told Simon what had happened. She put her arms around him and held on tightly. As if she could not bear to let him go.

Simon drew Shanti closer and ran his fingers through her long hair, spreading it like a dark veil over her shoulders.

'Shanti,' Simon murmured. 'What did you say it means—peace? That doesn't ring true at all. It should be something with more texture; a stormy sea, perhaps.'

Shanti told him her mother had given her the name. And he was right. It didn't fit. Just like the features that her mother had bestowed upon her hadn't replicated exactly either. While the little triangle of a nose, the bow-like mouth and large wide eyes composed a mask of serenity on her mother's face, they sat on Shanti like stormy clouds in volatile dissonance.

Simon told Shanti she could sleep in his house for what was left of the night. He drew back the curtains in his bedroom to let in the dawn.

Shanti touched Simon's face with her hands and ran her fingertips along his throat. She stroked the skin on his shoulders, the curves of his muscles, the fine hair on his forearms. She reached for his hands and interlaced her fingers with his. She looked up at Simon tentatively.

'You should get some sleep now,' Simon said to her.

Simon pulled back the blanket on his bed and made Shanti lie down. The rising sun touched Shanti's skin as Simon covered her with the blanket. He lay down next to her on top of the bedcover. He put one arm over her and fell into sleep easily. Shanti kept her eyes open, to catch each flicker of expression on his face. His arm felt warm through the blanket. Shanti felt as if she was diving into one of her dreams, but remained fully conscious.

She crawled closer to him and went to sleep, their limbs entangled in a web of bedclothes. It was late into the morning when Shanti woke. Simon was still fast asleep, his head nestled in the curve of her torso. His breath tickled her skin through the blanket between them as it rose and fell in an irregular pattern. She felt the hair on top of his head graze her chin, the steady rhythm of his heartbeat against her belly. He was smiling, a silly lopsided smile, as he continued to dream.

Shanti silently got out of bed, careful not to wake him. She leaned out of the bedroom window and plucked a flower from the hibiscus bush beneath. It was a full bloom, deep orange, flame red. She walked back to the bed and pressed her lips close to the edge of Simon's mouth. His stubble pricked her lips and made her draw back immediately. His floppy smile spread into a full-fledged grin. Shanti placed the flower on his pillow and left.

'Where have you been?' Shanti could feel droplets of Wairimu's saliva on her face as the housekeeper stood in front of her, blocking her way into the apartment.

'What does it matter to you, anyway,' Shanti said. She lifted her shoulders and dropped them to show that none of what Wairimu was saying was important to her.

'What did you say?' Wairimu pulled at the waistband of her apron as if she needed to do something to restrain herself.

'You knew,' Shanti said to Wairimu, not looking at her as she walked through the kitchen door. The accusation tumbled out of her.

'And what if I did?' Warimu turned to face Shanti.

'How could you let this happen to us?' Shanti stared at her in disbelief. 'After all that is between us. You let them come, thieves in the middle of the night, without warning us.'

It was Wairimu's turn to shrug. She looked steadily at Shanti and stated in a flat voice, 'Shanti, why do you refuse to understand? You know it is the way things happen here.'

'I'm going to my room. I want to call Mariella.' Shanti walked through the apartment with Wairimu following close behind.

'Yes, go and call your friend,' Wairimu said to the back of Shanti's head.

Wairimu had swept away the mess. Except for the broken portrait and damaged locks, there was no evidence of what had happened.

'In case you were wondering, your mother is still at the hospital.'

'Thanks to you,' Shanti said without turning around.

Wairimu grabbed Shanti by the elbow and forced her to turn around. She bent down so that their faces were almost touching. Shanti looked sideways, avoiding Wairimu's glare.

'You listen to me, girl,' Wairimu said. 'I told them not to touch your mother.'

'You told them!' Shanti sputtered. She was so angry she started to cry in front of Wairimu.

'Yes, I did. And it was better that I was in this. Have you seen what they did to the Shah family across the road?'

'How could you have been part of this?' Shanti whispered.

'It had to happen. Why can't you see these things, Shanti? You do not belong here.'

'I don't want to belong,' Shanti said, looking straight at Wairimu. 'I want to leave.'

'It is better that you go,' Wairimu said to Shanti. She shook her head and walked away.

Shanti wasn't allowed to see Mira until later that evening, during visiting hours. Mariella came over to spend the day with her.

'Do you think I did something really bad?' Shanti asked Mariella. giving up the pretence of going through past 'O' Level exam questions. She turned her chair away from the desk to face Mariella, who was lying on Shanti's bed with her eyes closed and her chemistry textbook resting on her thighs as she memorized the periodic table.

'No,' Mariella said. She opened her eyes to look at Shanti. 'Are you sure you didn't have sex with him?'

'I told you, I just slept in his bed.'

'That's nothing.' Mariella laughed. 'But don't tell your mother or that maid of yours, okay?'

'How can you be so calm about this?'

'Shanti, I'm going to tell you something I've never told anyone.' Mariella turned on her side to face Shanti.

'When we moved back to Uganda and I was sent to boarding school, the prefects used to punish us for whatever they liked. They'd make the boys stand naked and the girls in their swimming costumes, outside in the sun, to humiliate us. Once, I fainted and one of the prefects took me to his room. He told me I was a pain in the ass and that I never listened to any of the prefects. He said he'd make sure I wouldn't be punished any more if I had sex with him. So I did it. I guess everyone knew what happened; the girls wouldn't speak to me and they called me a prostitute to my face. My people have this problem... they are so bitter with life, maybe it's all those years of war, and they just don't like seeing others get a break from anything. So anyway, there was a lot of bad-mouthing and bitching and all. My brother told my parents and they took us both out of the school and sent us back to Nairobi. I hate him so much for telling them. My parents don't even look at me now. I know they don't respect me.'

Shanti looked at her hands that lay uselessly in her lap, wishing she knew how to tell Mariella that everything would be okay. She feigned a yawn.

'Are you tired?' Mariella asked. 'You can come here if you want.' She made space for Shanti on the bed.

Shanti lay down next to Mariella and put her arms around her. 'We have to get out of this place,' she whispered to her best friend.

'We will do it.'

'Yes, we'll pull off a disappearing act on everybody.'

'Is that a painting of you?' Mariella pointed at the wall above Shanti's bed.

'I suppose so. Flip made it. I think it looks more like my mother than me.'

'But you look like your mother,' Mariella said, digging her elbow into Shanti's ribs.

'Don't say that,' Shanti replied in a whisper. 'Look at her life. Look at what's happened.'

'Okay, I won't say it again,' Mariella said. 'Let's go to sleep now.'

'My poor mother,' Shanti said softly, more to herself than to Mariella.

Wairimu visited Mira in the hospital later that day. She wore a purple and magenta dress made of satin. It was similar to the dresses Mira had seen Wairimu wear many years ago, right after Prashant's death, when she'd discarded her uniform. The patent leather of her reddish-brown pumps matched her handbag. She had relaxed her hair and shaped it in a bouffant. Mira had never seen Wairimu wear lipstick before. She wondered if Wairimu had taken it from her dressing table before or after the break-in. As Wairimu stood in the hospital room, she seemed to take up all the empty space. The nurse on duty quickly left to get a padded armchair from the waiting room. The small wooden chair Shanti had sat in the night before would not do.

'So, they say you are sick,' Wairimu said to Mira after she had sat down and they had been left alone.

'Yes,' Mira replied. 'Very.'

'I thought they had fixed it when we let Shanti stay at the coast during the holidays.'

'There's more. They had to do a CT scan because of the cut on my head. It is in my brain now. Maybe it always was. But they found it this time.'

'How come they cannot fix it again?'

'I would have to go abroad. It costs too much, and there's no guarantee that they can fix it.'

'I am sorry,' Wairimu said. Her voice remained flat. 'How long will it be?'

'It will be soon.'

'And what is going to happen to Shanti?'

'I asked Lata to call Prashant's relatives in Vancouver. They will be her guardians. She will stay one year with them to finish school. Then she can apply to university in Canada. That country has money for their residents to go to college.'

'You cannot take care of her education there?'

'No, Wairimu, I never could. You think Prashant's Kenyan shillings are worth anything abroad? We never had that kind of money. He was not one of the corrupt ones who had stolen money that was not his. You refused to believe me. I did what I could with his savings for the retirement plans for you and Samuel. And for all of us by getting this apartment when we lost that house he worked so hard to buy. You think Lata gave me this apartment for free? I don't know what you think we're made of.' Mira started laughing. It went out of control and ended up in tears. 'You probably had more than we did before the attack. But you know you will have more after it.'

Wairimu shifted in her chair. She had nothing to say.

'You will have the apartment as well. Or at least the debt I've been carrying, trying to buy it slowly,' Mira said. 'I was planning on giving it to you, anyway. It's what I have said in my will. What use is it to Shanti? It translates into nothing over there. She'll have to make her own way. The apartment will only keep her tied to this place. Her studies will make her depend less on the kindness of others. It is more than what I had, at least. And

I thought it was more than you had. But you, you turned out to be different from what I thought.'

'I didn't want it to happen like this,' Wairimu said. 'You must understand.' Her eyes implored Mira.

'It is done,' Mira said. She couldn't bring herself to look at her housekeeper.

Shanti almost walked into Wairimu while the older woman was leaving. They did not address each other.

'How could you let that woman come to see you?' This was the first thing that came out of Shanti's mouth.

'Shanti, please. There are things you will never understand.' Mira closed her eyes. 'And there are more important things I have to speak to you about.'

'Oh, ma,' Shanti said. 'I'm sorry.'

'There is nothing for you to be sorry about. You must remember that. There are things that have been happening to me that I have been hiding from you.'

'Ma, please tell me what's happening.'

'It is I who should be pleading with you,' said Mira.

Mira felt as if her heart was breaking all over again. She let out a long, drawn-out breath that would pass for a sigh if it were not so laboured. She looked through the open door of her room, out at the corridor, away from Shanti, and began to speak.

'Let's see. About eight months ago, I noticed I was eating more than usual but was losing weight. I also noticed a hernia-type lump in my abdomen but ignored it longer than I should have. Oh, and there was always that fatigue. I was always tired, forever sleeping. I never could get enough rest.'

Shanti could not believe what she was hearing. She wanted to close her ears, shut out her mother's voice.

'After a few months of waiting, I decided to see a doctor. He told me I had cysts and that he would have to operate. We scheduled it when you were away on your school trip. On the day of the surgery, I didn't feel frightened or nervous but I did have a feeling of dread: call it your mother's intuition. But they said the surgery went well.'

'You should have told me,' Shanti said. She could not keep the accusation out of her voice.

'I should have told you? You were having fun, at last, with your friend. I didn't want to burden you. I kept up the pretence of believing your silly excuses about staying longer at the coast. It was better for me to have more time to recover. Shanti, you seemed so happy. I couldn't take that away from you. Maybe it was the wrong decision.'

'What's going to happen now?' Shanti asked, her voice low, the only way it could be at that moment. 'Ma, please tell me the truth.'

'They've found a brain tumor. It's been there for a long time. They say they can see it now.' Mira's voice broke.

'I don't understand. What happens next?'

'I come home. Then it will be the end for me.'

Shanti could not see because of the tears, so many tears, blurring the image of her mother lying against the pillows. She could not think. She tried to make sense of the matter that had been presented before her. 'Ma, shouldn't we consider the alternatives? Surgery? Isn't there more information we can get on these things?'

'Shanti, all these experts have their own opinions about dealing with my condition but I will do it my way. At home. My doctor has agreed. I hope you understand.'

The nurse walked into the room, moving about like a shadow, an omen that augured the end. Her pastel uniform and cheery voice made a mockery of Mira's condition, as if it were a coincidence that she was there, that she just happened to be present at the incident of Mira's decline. There was a multitude of ways in which Shanti wanted to respond. But she ended up saying nothing. She knew she had no more say in the matter. It was settled.

21

THE FIRST FEW DAYS after Mira returned home passed uneventfully. Her level of pain was controlled with medication. Shanti first prowled around her like a caged animal. But when Mira suggested that Shanti call Mariella over or retrieve a pain pill for her, she realized her mother was asking to be left alone. For space to breathe. They settled into a routine. Every morning they drank their tea together. Shanti had decided not to go to school that week and no one commented on it. The evenings were quiet, spent outside on the verandah, reading. Both Flip and Carol visited when they returned to the compound and heard what had happened.

Carol told them she had gone to her father's house near Lake Victoria over the weekend. Her husband wanted to move into one of her father's properties and work with him to secure his place in the next election. Carol had agreed to leave the city and her job, and move back into one of her father's houses with her husband. Her husband had agreed to keep trying to have children with her.

'I'm a professor married to a politician, and look at me—after all this education and training, I have been reduced to nothing. I can't even get pregnant,' Carol said. 'That is why I agreed to leave my job and have us move back with my family. Look at Ben, who made so much fun of my father. He wants it all. Everything my father has. They get along so well now.'

'How are you going to keep trying to have children?' Flip asked Carol.

'We're trying in vitro. We tried before, in South Africa. We're going to a clinic in London this time. It's my fault, you know, I have holes in my Fallopian tubes. Everything drains through them like a sieve.' She forced a smile. 'And Ben must have his own children. You know what our men are like. He even suggested asking a family friend to make a baby with him. With our traditions, that would entitle her to become his second wife. With her children, she could probably take my place.'

'You must not allow that,' Mira said with a fierceness that startled them all.

'I still think you should leave him,' Flip said.

'It is not that easy, Flip. We are not like you,' Carol said. 'I do not know one white settler who does not come from some sort of a broken home.'

'We'll figure something out, Carol. You mustn't worry,' Mira said. She squeezed her friend's hand.

'We're not that different, you know,' Flip said. 'I was upcountry over the weekend as well. My family needs to sell our farm to a politician there. Maybe your family knows him, Carol?' Flip could not keep the sarcasm out of her voice.

Carol did not respond. She kept her eyes on Mira, for whom they were both there.

'My family is moving to South Africa. I'm going with them. There's nothing left for me here,' Flip continued.

'What happened to that mzungu ranch owner you had your eyes on?' Carol asked in an attempt to mend the rift.

'He's in jail. He shot a Samburu hunter on his land by accident.'

'How do your people shoot so many Africans by accident, Flip?' Carol asked, irritation creeping into her voice again.

'I don't know, Carol,' Flip's temper flared. 'How do your people manage to shoot so many of us on purpose? Bloody hell, we need to get out of this country just to stay alive.'

Flip's poky body floated somewhere inside the orange pantaloons and baggy sweater she always wore. She looked like a street urchin. Shanti watched the back of her shorn head, silvery tufts of hair stuck out forlornly, casting curious shadows on the wall in front of her as she stared straight ahead without looking at Carol. Shanti couldn't imagine Flip living anywhere else. She would belong in Johannesburg as much as Shanti would belong in Vancouver.

'Wait. What's happening?' Mira said, confused. 'When are you leaving?'

'We will stay for as long as you are here,' Carol replied. She looked at Flip. 'But let us go today, Mira. You're tired, you must rest.'

After Shanti had seen her mother's friends to the door, Wairimu came out of the kitchen.

'Heh! These people have no idea. They think their lives are so sad. And where do you think Carol got the money for her baby-making procedures? She stole it from the university. You think she is leaving by choice? She was sacked. That woman and her husband need her father's big-man shadow to protect them. And Flip? She knows we do not need any mzungus owning our land any more.'

'I am not interested in your opinions about other people, Wairimu,' Shanti told her. 'Please. I do not want to talk any more.'

'You suit yourself,' Wairimu said before she went back into the kitchen. 'I am here because your mother wants me here.'

The break-in had altered the relationship between Wairimu and the Sharmas, mother and daughter alike. Both sides took great pains to protect themselves against any further infidelity.

They no longer allowed themselves to share their interests, the intimate details of their personal lives and family histories. There were no discussions on different spiritual beliefs, gossip over friends and neighbours, confessions about lovers and children. There was no more laughter heard from the kitchen, no more stories shared.

—

Shanti sneaked out with Mariella to visit a bar in a suburb of Nairobi. It was a Thursday night and they were in Westlands. On their drive there, Shanti saw the complicated character of the area. At first glance it appeared residential, but commercial buildings had sprung up in a haphazard manner, the roads winding around them displayed seamier sides to the town.

They sat outside, at a table close to the pavement. They were joined by Matthew, an Australian with the embassy who knew one of Mariella's older brothers and had stayed at their home, though Mariella had been bribed by her brother not to tell their parents; and Matthew's friend, Carlos, a filmmaker from Argentina who was in Nairobi to shoot a documentary. There was constant traffic as clusters of adolescents and pre-teens made their way to and from the bar, the casino next door and a club on the other side of the highway. All three places accepted anyone, regardless of age. There were a few prostitutes who looked as if they were still girls, sitting at the bar inside. Foreign men stood at the periphery, hovering before them as they waited for the appropriate moment to settle a transaction. Shanti noticed Sebu sitting at a table next to the bar. A girl straddled his lap, kissing him.

There was a long silence, and Shanti realized they were all waiting for her to respond.

'Oh,' she said, startled, blurting out an explanation in an effort to make up for her rudeness. 'Everyone thought my mother was crazy, but she's not. She has a brain tumor.'

She started to giggle and then stopped abruptly, her laughter evaporating as quickly as it had appeared. She let another silence, more stunned this time, hang over them as she took a few more sips of her second drink.

'I'm so sorry,' said Carlos finally.

'I must leave,' Shanti said. She felt mysteriously elated as she stood up. Mariella followed her as she started to walk away.

'What's wrong with you?' Mariella asked. 'You're the one acting crazy.'

'Mariella, don't talk to me like that,' Shanti replied. She had drunk two gin-and-tonics and knew she was overreacting. She turned to look at the bar again.

'Don't be fussed,' Mariella said, putting her arm around Shanti. 'Sebu's just getting off with the mzungu girl because he can. They're like that, as you know very well.'

'It's different with me and Simon,' Shanti said. 'I told you, nothing happened. You won't understand.' Intimating confidence about the existence of a relationship outside the one between them was a luxury. An extravagance she was too ill-equipped to afford. Exhibitionism, perhaps only poor judgement in a more stable world, became a serious breach when people thought you were taking too many liberties. Shanti felt she'd left herself open to Mariella, mirroring her mother and Lata in some ways, allowing herself to be gutted through if her friend decided to move in for the kill.

Shanti walked down the road to look for a taxi, anxious to get away. She suddenly noticed that she had headed down an unlit street. Darkness surrounded her in varying densities. She heard a man and a woman talking a few paces ahead. Then there was another noise, sounds that were not words. She tried to move away as silently and as quickly as possible, afraid that if she was discovered, they might have to do something awful to her, whether they wanted to or not. This was not the kind of city where people were at ease when discovered in illicit circumstances.

The couple broke away and the taller figure, a white man, came towards her. 'You looking for something, love?' the man said to her. The young African girl he was with crouched into the darkness.

Shanti hurriedly explained that she was looking for a cab. The man waved her in the direction of a hotel. Shanti ran all the way there and found taxis parked outside.

—

Mira watched Shanti's every move as she pottered about in the room. There was a tension between them today that Shanti could not fully grasp. Shanti thought back over their recent interactions. She replayed every conversation, every mood, every dose of medication. At each turn, she came up empty-handed.

Shanti carried out sundry inconsequential tasks in her mother's small room: she arranged and re-arranged the flowers Flip had put on the bedside table; she sorted through the library books that Carol had brought for Mira, checking and re-checking their due dates; she folded Mira's clothes, smoothed the bedspread and fluffed up the pillows as Mira continued to stare at Shanti from within that heavy silence.

'I don't know how much longer I want to live like this.' Mira hesitated for a moment and then added, with an edge of irrevocability to her voice, 'I've asked Mercilene to make something for me.'

Shanti did not say a word. The raw certitude of her mother's decision reached into her, contracting and dividing her flesh as it burrowed into her heart. The medicine woman would give Mira something so she would no longer live. Shanti forced herself to understand: her mother had lived like this, like an invalid, for too long. Shanti looked at Mira helplessly, unable to speak.

Mira told Shanti she had received a letter from Vijay Sharma, Prashant's brother in Vancouver, and he had said that Shanti could stay with them. The schooling would be free and the rest of Prashant's savings would give her an allowance, enough to spend on food and clothes for a few years. She could get into a good university with subsidy and work on campus to earn some money. Vijay's children were both in college. He and his wife had place for her in their house. They were happy to have her. It was the best outcome. Mira didn't want Shanti to spend the rest of her life here.

Mira told Shanti she needed to make sure Wairimu and Samuel were satisfied with their life-earnings. Wairimu had spent her savings on the house she'd built in her village, and Samuel, Mira was certain, had drunk his away. There was no more money to give them. Mira asked Shanti if Samuel could inherit the car and Wairimu the apartment. Otherwise, both would belong to Shanti.

It no longer mattered what Wairimu did or did not get. Shanti did not wish to remain here, in this place so laden with memory.

After they had discussed these practicalities, these details of miniscule proportion that seemed to have burgeoned into stupendous, distinct lives of their own as mother and daughter treated each with utmost care, Shanti and Mira were at a complete loss for conversation. Mira sank into the bedsheets, exhausted. She had expended every ounce of energy within her.

She had said everything she needed to say. It was late and Mira wanted Shanti to leave so she could rest. Shanti could hear the crickets chirping outside. They sounded eerily animated from within her mother's dark room.

Shanti stopped going to school altogether. She told Mira that she no longer had to take her 'O' Level exams if a place was already secured for her in the high school in Canada. Her uncle had sent a course catalogue for the International Baccalaureate at the school in his neighbourhood. Shanti borrowed textbooks from the library at the Canadian consulate and stayed at home and studied by herself during the day so she could be near Mira.

A week and a half after she stopped going to school, Simon came to see Shanti. They went for a walk. Simon took a small object out of his pocket and handed it to Shanti. It was a lumpy frog made out of banana fibre. Shanti looked over the crudely woven coir that concocted the misshapen creature, the chips of coloured glass that served as bulging eyes, the contorted beam of thin wire that was patchily glued onto its face to form a crooked smile. It was truly the ugliest creature ever wrought by man, nature or machine. Shanti thought it was the nicest gift anyone had ever given her.

'I bought it on my way here, from one of the street kids hawking stuff through the traffic,' Simon explained offhandedly, running his fingers through his hair.

'It is lovely.' Shanti smiled. 'Thank you.'

'It's actually from all of us at school. We miss you. Many of the girls, not just Mariella. And the boys on the hockey team,' Simon tilted his head sideways for effect. 'Especially the captain.'

'I'm done with all that.' Shanti couldn't help blushing. After a moment, she said, 'They don't play this kind of hockey in

Canada, do they?' She told him about the plans for her to live with her uncle and his family in Vancouver.

Dark clouds, pregnant with rain, were suspended over the city like a great shift in the sky. The short rains were almost upon them.

'The promise of rain,' said Simon as he breathed in the moist air. 'It was always so hot and dry when I was up north at the camp.'

'You've never talked to any of us about your time spent at the border.'

'I thought I'd be prepared for it. I'm a doctor, after all. But it was a completely different arena for death. You students can't understand how bad things are there.'

'I can,' Shanti said. 'I haven't told you everything about what's going to happen to my mother. I can understand many things.'

'Okay, I'll tell you what happened,' said Simon. Shanti wished he would stop smiling like he thought it his duty to encourage her inquiries about how the world worked. 'There was an incident. I spent my time there treating refugees, soldiers, rebels, anyone who needed medical attention and could make it to the clinic that had been set up at the border. We were set up very close to the battles, in Bulo Hawa in the Gedo region, just five hundred metres from the border. One evening, just as I was packing up for the day, a group of soldiers came into the clinic. The soldiers were more like children with guns, I don't know which faction they belonged to, probably some marauding clan-based militia, mooryan raiders, I'd stopped trying to figure out the different affiliations by then. They had four patients for me. They ordered me to make sure the men survived the night.'

'How old were the children?' Shanti asked Simon. 'When I went with Wairimu to her village, we saw all these children with AIDS—they looked as if they were three or four years old.'

'I think these children were between twelve and sixteen-seventeen.'

Shanti gave him a look.

'Sorry,' Simon replied. 'They were young adults. Like you.'

'Anyway, what was wrong with the patients they had brought to you?'

'They were wounded. Badly. Gunshots, stabbings, lacerations, burns. It wasn't difficult to see that they had been tortured.'

'How many of them died?' Shanti asked Simon abruptly.

Simon looked confused. After a moment, he continued.

'One of them, a bearded young man who couldn't have been more than eighteen, had been blinded and he had cuts all over his body, as if he had been beaten with a machete. Part of his face was burnt. He was still conscious and pleaded with me to end his life. I have never seen anyone so wretched, so broken, so terrified of living, so eager to die.'

'Did you help him?' Shanti asked, afraid of what she was going to hear.

'I did. I helped him die and told the soldiers that there was nothing I could have done to save him.'

'Then what happened?' Shanti said, trying to keep her voice level.

'Later that night, I was woken by someone shaking me. The soldiers were in my tent. They made me go outside. Out of the campgrounds and into the open dark. I was barefoot and kept stumbling. They threatened me, saying I should have obeyed their orders. Then they stripped me and made me walk back naked to the clinic. They followed me most of the way, their rifles pointing at my back as they asked me all sorts of things—whether I wanted to be famous for being the Jesus of Africa or if I thought I was bloody Mother Teresa. It was almost dawn then and a few people saw me—some guards, a few of the relief workers. I said I had stupidly left the camp grounds for a walk during the night and had been robbed. I'm sure everyone knew that wasn't true. They must have had some idea about what had happened, but no one said or did anything. In the morning, back at the clinic, the other three patients were gone. I thought I heard shrieking during the day but no one else seemed to notice.'

'What do you mean, shrieking?'

'I mean screams of torture. But I really can't be certain. Fear produces a pretty overactive imagination, you know. Anyway, it was so very quiet afterwards, so still. I don't know if I imagined the whole thing. Later in the afternoon, a crowd gathered outside the camp in this open area we had cleared of brush, where we sometimes lit bonfires. I walked over and saw three bodies hanging from a large tree. I can still see them swaying back and forth, even though there was no wind. The heat was always so bloody stifling. As for the entire camp, I don't know what happened to them. They acted as if there was a fucking parade being held for their entertainment. Every single person—refugee, relief worker, soldier—just stood there, gaping at the three dead men. Those bodies were my patients from the night before. The story was that they had committed suicide.'

'What did you do?'

'Nothing. I kept my head down and completed the rest of my time and then packed my bags and came to Nairobi. I'd like to believe I did some good by treating anyone in need, regardless of their position, but it's difficult to operate from a theoretically neutral platform when you're in the middle of a war.'

Shanti didn't know what to say. She could feel her emotions swirling around her, as inviting as a rain-bearing wind. She wished she could do something, say something that would make everything okay.

'My mother is going to die,' Shanti said quietly. 'She has asked the medicine woman in our compound to give her something. She wants to die. I mean, she's already dying...'

Simon took Shanti's hand in his. 'I'm very sorry,' he said.

'I want to leave straight after it happens,' Shanti told him.

After a long moment, Simon said, 'I can't really imagine what it will be like to get back to my old life in London. It was always so well defined, a solid future guarded safely by strong walls. So different from anything here.'

Shanti wondered if she would be able to stay in touch with Simon, or with anyone here.

'I'll write to you,' he said, answering her thoughts with a certainty she could not feel.

When she turned towards him, she could see the complicated future she had waiting ahead, the painful memories that would reside in the corners of her life.

'Amygdala,' Simon said as he reached over and placed a closed fist on Shanti's forehead.

'Are you performing African medicine on me to cure me of my ailments?' she asked, smiling in spite of herself.

'No,' Simon replied. 'Amygdala is the part of your brain that produces and responds to fear, dark memories, dreams. It is almond-shaped, like your beautiful eyes.'

Shanti raised her eyebrows. Simon shrugged, giving her an apologetic smile.

'Well, anyway, we don't know a lot about it. But recent breakthroughs in amygdala research have enhanced our understanding of why and how human beings feel various emotions and remember emotional situations, especially fearful ones.'

'Is that what the doctors would have looked at in my mother if we lived abroad?'

'A connection has been made between the basic neurobiology of the amygdala in a human being and his or her propensity to experience debilitating socio-emotional disorders. But we're not very developed in our thinking in this area, here or abroad.'

'The doctors here say it's too late to help my mother,' Shanti said. 'But we could use the money we have to send her overseas instead of me. If only she would agree.'

'It does seem like what the doctors are saying is right. That the tumor is inoperable.' They continued walking, climbing up a hill that was on the way to Shanti's old primary school. They were surrounded by dark green trees and misty skies. They both stopped when they reached the top of the hill. The entire grey-green landscape was covered with luminescent lilac splashes—the jacaranda flowers had made their brief annual appearance throughout the city.

Simon held Shanti as she let the tears roll down her face and spill onto him. It was sufficient to live through each day, through each life even, and sporadically, sparsely, perceive such astonishing beauty. Not too often, as its clarity pierced through the soul, but intermittently, in small measure.

'It is so perfect,' said Shanti, shuddering as she rested her head against Simon's shoulder. 'My memories of this place should only be like this.'

They walked back through the gardens surrounding the apartment building. It was dusk. The sun was settling, setting the flame trees on fire as it descended. Shanti could hear the fireflies buzzing in the air as they waited for the rain.

'In the end, after all this is over, it—you—will be all right,' Simon said.

'Okay,' Shanti replied, trying to sound assured about how things might play out, despite her own apprehensions.

It was dark now, amalgamating a restless night. Shanti could hear intimations of life rustling through the grass, in the air and among the leaves. They were standing under a moonflower tree,close to the gates of the compound. The hanging trumpet-shaped flowers were luminous in the evening and their sweet aura spread over Shanti and Simon.

Simon reached up and plucked a perfect, pendent bloom. He tried to fix it in Shanti's hair. The soft white petals disintegrated, leaving fragments of the flower's skin and its scent lingering in her hair and on his fingers.

Flip and Lata were still with Mira when Simon and Shanti returned. Perhaps it was just Shanti's imagination but the apartment had begun to take on a musty smell—as if it were crumbling under the weight of regret, a repository of lost time. Shanti quickly lit an incense cone under the broken frame of her father's portrait , inhaling deep breaths of the smoked scent of jasmine.

Flip emerged from Mira's bedroom. Her eyes were so swollen they looked as if they were about to explode.

'Oh, Flip,' Shanti said as she put her arms around her mother's friend. Flip's usually sprite body drooped as she began to sob.

'Look.' Her voice was wobbly as she wept into Shanti's shoulder. 'We've decided to have a dinner party. It was Wairimu's idea. We just set the date with Mira.'

Shanti agreed at once, ignoring Wairimu who was looking at Shanti over Flip's crumpled frame.

'Are you sure it's a good idea?' Simon asked Shanti as soon as Flip had gone.

Shanti could hear the legitimate concern in Simon's voice. 'They want to do something for my mother,' she told him with a confidence that rang so sincere it surprised them both. The answer had come to her like a ripple of water, so clearly not her own that Shanti knew it was the right decision.

When Lata came out of Mira's room, Shanti expected to see the usual storm of melodrama, the martyr-like sighs and self-pitying sobs. But there was none. Instead, a rough, grainy sorrow was etched into her dimpled cheeks, making her look very old.

Shanti began to console Lata with words she found herself repeating so many times they inadvertently came out in a monotonous robotic stream. The pity Shanti could see in Lata's eyes choked her into silence. It was only when Lata spoke that Shanti perceived the depth of kindness that was within her, the genuine warmth in her heart that lay underneath all that affectation, that had made Mira form such a close friendship with this woman.

'Now, beti, you must let me take care of the food for this dinner party.' She surprised Shanti all over again. Her voice was smooth and strong with a sincerity that Shanti never thought she possessed.

When Shanti was about to decline her offer, Lata cut her off, her eyes twinkling as she wagged her finger at her. 'You and Wairimu will have your hands full, taking care of everything else. And anyway, who else but me knows where to get the best pakoras and kachoris in town?'

Shanti did not even realize she was crying until Lata wiped the tears off her face and embraced her, covering her with comfort.

'Who will I have to look after me?' Lata said suddenly, sitting down on the chair closest to her. 'Your mother is very lucky.'

'I'm sure the community will provide, Lata aunty,' Shanti said simply, 'when it's your time.'

Lata clapped and flapped her hands about her head and shoulders and knocked on the wooden arms of her chair. It was a fervent attempt to avail herself of a medley of eastern and western remedies in order to ward off any spirits bearing ill-fate who might decide to test Shanti's assertion. Shanti started laughing at Lata, who looked as if she was trying to swat away a swarm of invisible flies that had suddenly descended on her.

—

The short rains had finally arrived. Shanti sat bundled up in a shawl on the verandah and watched the large raindrops splatter onto the earth. They made large puddles on the surface of the pool and clung to the hibiscus flowers like small darts. She could hear the fireflies stirring in the air. It would be impossible to sit out on the patio at night. As Shanti sat there, looking outside, like every other resident before her, she saw her own potential, her future. Her desire to sustain attachments to people, to create a sense of place was futile. Things had changed along with the value she ascribed to them. Shanti found herself longing for her life away from Kenya, seeking comfort in its simplicity and the clear set of rules it would allow her to live by. She had no part in this land. Shanti felt relief at leaving this place of overpowering ambiguity to her memories, turning away from its chorus of familiar faces as mere shadows of a life past. She was now certain that was where they all truly belonged—in her dreams.

She trundled to the car, still wrapped in the now soaked pashmina. The driveway was more like a rivulet with all the water streaming over it. Once inside the car, Shanti emerged from her soft, damp cocoon, only to be hit by an onslaught of cold, musky air. She saw Samuel in the rearview mirror. He was standing near the gate with the new askari, looking relaxed, laughing and talking. They were holding two mugs that Samuel had brought out from the apartment. Shanti could just about see the askari pour an amber liquid from a small plastic packet into both mugs.

Samuel joined her in the car after he finished his drink. As they drove past the bougainvillea-covered fence, Shanti noticed Samuel's hands quivering against the wheel. Shanti decided not to comment on it.

Shanti met Mariella at Trattoria, an Italian restaurant in the centre of town. She ordered a cappuccino and sipped it slowly while Mariella tucked away copious amounts of gelato. Shanti told her that they had heard from her uncle in Canada.

'Great. Do you think it'll be like *Sixteen Candles*?' Mariella said, not looking up from her dessert.

'I hope not.' Shanti sighed. 'Anyway, that's the United States, not Canada.'

Mariella's head snapped up from her ice-cream. 'It is all America.'

Shanti sighed again. 'I'll miss you. Who will you hang out with at school when I'm gone?'

'Actually, I've been meaning to tell you,' Mariella said casually. 'We're leaving too. My parents are taking us back to Kampala. I don't have to do the O's either. They say things are good now.'

'What? How can they send you back to Uganda after what happened?'

Mariella frowned and Shanti wished she hadn't said anything.

After a moment, Mariella said, 'I don't care. It must be better than it is here. You're lucky you are leaving, Shanti.'

'Maybe we'll just be apart for a year,' Shanti said. 'We can go to the same university in Canada. We'll apply to the same places.'

Mariella laughed. 'You really think it's as easy as that?' She reached over and yanked at Shanti's long hair, pulling her closer.

'Ow, stop!' Shanti didn't like the fact that she couldn't hold and pull Mariella's hair, a reminder of the difference between them. She reached over and dug her nails into Mariella's arm until her friend let go of her hair.

'Well, at least the dreamer has talons,' Mariella said, settling back into her chair. 'You'll need them in America.'

'Ya, because you know so much about everything, as usual,' Shanti replied.

'More than you, my friend.' Mariella laughed again. 'More than you.'

'So I'll see you at this dinner party we're having for my mother?' Shanti tried to change the subject.

Mariella did not reply.

'It'll be our farewell dinner as well,' Shanti said. 'Anyway, you know I need you there.'

Mariella grinned. 'Then I'll be there for sure.'

The afternoon was frenetic when Shanti stepped out of the dark restaurant. The road outside was teeming with honking cars, harried businessmen, bellowing hawkers and beggars. She shielded her eyes against the sun-filled vista and searched for Samuel.

Samuel waved to Shanti from the far end of the street. As she walked towards him, a boy who didn't look as if he was older than ten swaggered up to her. His thin chest was barely concealed by a tattered white shirt that he wore over a pair of stained khaki shorts. His eyes were open unnaturally wide, his pupils looked dilated, the cornea more red than white. He held a broken Coca-Cola bottle in his hand.

Samuel rushed at him, waving his arms and yelling, 'Weh, kwenda! Leave her alone!'

Samuel and Shanti got into the car and Samuel made sure all the doors were locked and the windows rolled up. He was still clicking his tongue against his teeth in irritation when he settled into the driver's seat and fastened his seatbelt.

'Samuel,' Shanti said. 'It's okay. He wasn't bothering me. He's just a kid.'

'Eh, no, Shanti, you cannot even trust these watotos any more.'

'Why was he stumbling?'

'He is high on glue. Nowadays that is all they do.'

'What happened to the city council schools that were set up in town?'

'They do not want to go to school. Heh, they are thieves. All they want is money, the children to sniff glue, the parents to drink changaa and who knows what else? They do not want to work. They are all heathens.' The old driver made this pronouncement dismissively with a grand sweep of his arm.

Shanti said nothing and focused on changing the gears for Samuel instead.

22

THE SMALL KITCHEN WAS iridescent. It glistened with vegetables and meat sizzling in pots and pans of varied sizes. The utensils were constantly being shifted on and off the stove as if they were engaged in a game of musical chairs. There was too much clutter across the countertop—chopped onions, diced tomatoes, julienned peppers and a collage of spices. There were too many bodies.

'Shanti, who told you to put the chicken in already? The masala isn't cooked yet,' Wairimu said.

'It was sticking to the non-stick sufuria, okay?'

'You two, I can smell something burning,' Mira piped up from her post in the large chair that Wairimu and Shanti had dragged into the kitchen from the verandah. 'Oh, oh, and I can see something bubbling over on the stove.'

'Shit, it's the rice. Ma, where is the saffron?'

'Wairimu will show you.'

'Take these strawberries away, Shanti. I need space to roll out the paranthas.'

'I need them to make the dessert which, by the way, I can't do right now because the butter's in the fridge and your chair's blocking the fridge door, ma,' Shanti said distractedly as she heaved the pot of rice off the stove. 'Ma?'

'Your mother is sleeping.'

'Why is she always dozing off like that? It must be a side-effect. But the doctor didn't warn us about it.'

'The doctors, they know nothing.'

'That's not true.'

'Heh, I know it in my heart. And I can see it is all true anyway.'

Shanti caught herself sliding into the familiar banter with Wairimu. It was still so easy, even after everything that had happened between them.

'Can I just turn on the oven to bake my strawberries, please?'

'Tcha! I have never seen people cook strawberries.'

'I told you. It's a recipe I found in a Canadian magazine at the consulate.'

'I'm sure it will be delicious, darling,' Mira's soothing voice drifted towards Shanti through the scrim of steam hanging over the stove.

After the badaam chicken, saag paneer, gobi mattar, paranthas, saffron rice and baked strawberries had all been prepared, Wairimu and Shanti turned to decorating the house for the evening. The apartment was transformed. Wairimu and Shanti lined the hallway, every windowsill and balcony with diyas.

Shanti walked out to the garden and picked flowers. She arranged jasmine flowers in a vase and placed it under her father's portrait in the hallway. She wished she had asked Flip to fix the frame before people saw it in the evening. It was still cracked, a constant reminder of the break-in. In the centre of the dining table, she set a cut-glass bowl, given to them for the occasion by Carol. She filled it with water and carefully decorated it with floating candles. She scattered rose petals around the bowl. Petals from the rose garden outside Mira's bedroom window. The same roses Mira wanted her ashes to be scattered over. Even in her death, she wanted to assist the little patch of earth she had so diligently cultivated during her better days, so she could attempt to grow another season of exquisite blooms. Shanti tried to picture Lata aunty's reaction to this and smiled. She still hadn't told Wairimu that Lata was bringing food for dinner as well. She didn't have the energy to break that kind of news to Wairimu, and hoped that things would somehow sort themselves out, or that the two women would battle it out in the kitchen while her mother and the guests were safely out of the way in the living room.

Mira sat on the sofa, her feet resting on a cushioned stool. Less than an hour ago, Shanti had bathed her and washed her hair. They agreed upon an embroidered kaftan for Mira to wear, which would serve as elegant eveningwear while offering her the comfort of a nightgown. Mira had let Shanti line her eyes with kohl and clasp a necklace around her neck that Flip had made for her, inset with pieces of glass the colour of diamonds and emeralds. Even though it was a warm night, Shanti needed to wrap a shawl around Mira to ease her shivering.

The guests arrived.

Carol brought a bouquet of flowers instead of her absent husband. She also brought a jar of honey, collected from the beehives on her father's property where they now lived, and a carved wooden spatula inlaid with ivory, to scoop out the honey.

Simon came alone with a bottle of wine in hand.

Flip carried another portrait she had painted of Shanti at the behest of Mira, the image was yet another reflection of her mother, not of herself, Shanti felt, but said nothing.

Lata rushed in, breathless, spilling out her tale du jour (she was certain the deputy high commissioner's wife was shagging the embassy doctor while shamelessly masquerading as a chaste Hindu woman). Mohan followed Lata. Following Lata's husband was her driver, carrying a kikapu filled with things for dinner.

'My, Shanti, you look all grown up in maroon and gold.'

'Thank you, I'm wearing one of ma's saris.'

Lata aimed lateral kisses at the space between Shanti's cheek and shoulder.

'But your poor mother looks so tiny, sitting on that sofa. It just makes me want to cry.'

'She looks wonderful,' Carol cut in.

Shanti hugged Carol gratefully as she took the flowers from her, 'Roses! My mother's favourite. I'll place them before the fireplace. We thought it was too warm to light a fire this evening.'

'Flip, your hair has a purple tinge,' Carol exclaimed.

'Yes, my darling. It is to embrace the warm Bacchanalian night we have ahead of us.'

'Well, go show it to ma. She'll love it.'

'Shanti, I sneaked a peek in the kitchen. Did you really cook all that?'

'Shanti, Lata was right. You are now a spitting image of your mother when she first came to Africa.'

'Shanti, you look, well, you look great.'

'Simon, thank you. I'm so glad you could come.'

After the guests filed past her, Shanti looked out of the front door. Mariella had not yet arrived.

'Please sit down, everyone. I'm feeling quite left out, sitting here by myself on this big sofa.'

There was a surge of collective guilt as everyone rushed to join Mira.

Mira was too tired to have all these people buzzing around her, but the desire to keep them near was stronger. Her face radiated happiness as they gathered around.

'Flippa, this portrait of Shanti is splendid!' Mira said.

'Doesn't it have more of my mother in it than it does of me?'

'Shanti, honestly, how could Flip or anyone else paint a picture of you without your mother in it?'

'Yes, Shanti, go look in the mirror and then at the picture of your parents on the mantelpiece.'

'No, no, not the one by where Simon is sitting. The wedding picture where you look just like your mother.'

'Oho! Don't scare the poor girl. No daughter likes to hear she looks just like her mother.'

'No, that's not what I meant at all...'

'Well, accept it, girl, you are your mother.'

'Ahem, on that note, I'd like to propose a toast in honour of the man who is not with us today in person. Yet he is surely here, looking at us from the portrait in the hallway, in this very room and in my heart. Shanti, my dear girl, with all this talk of you being the identical image of your mother, I must say I see a good part of your father in you as well. In memory of my dear friend, Prashant Sharma.'

The rest of them raised their glasses to Mohan Patel, who looked quite solemn, standing in the middle of the room, silhouetted by the light of the oil lamps.

In addition to some dishes, Lata had brought a tablecloth and silverware to use for the party.

Wairimu whispered furiously to Shanti, 'Does that woman think our things are not good enough to use? I will throw out the food she has brought.'

'No,' Shanti said. 'We must serve her food and use the dinnerware. Anyway, her things are nicer than ours.'

'Since when have you become so friendly with that woman?'

'She's brought all this for ma,' Shanti replied.

Wairimu and Shanti laid out the food buffet-style on the dining table. Shanti took her mother's usual place at the head of the table and handed each guest a plate, cutlery and a lace napkin as they began to serve themselves.

'Yes, can you imagine, all this time the brazen witch was recommending him as the world's best physician because she had something going on with him,' said Lata as she took a plate from Shanti. 'And it was all taking place in the embassy house under her husband's nose!'

'Oh my,' was all Carol offered Lata in response.

'Well, at least she's getting a good prod and a poke whenever she visits her doctor, if you know what I mean,' chimed in Flip as she nudged Lata in her well-cushioned ribs. 'Wow, what a fantastic spread!'

After the women had served themselves, Simon and Mohan walked to the dining table.

'No, no, Shanti, after you, I insist,' Mohan protested when Shanti offered him a plate.

'Oh, all right, let's serve ourselves together, Mohan uncle.'

Simon took two plates, one in each hand, and turned to Shanti. 'Why don't we serve your mother's portion as well. It'll save you a trip.'

Shanti wondered if she was the only one who had noticed one remaining plate on the table. She took the empty plate back to the kitchen and packed it away in Lata's kikapu, deciding that Mariella was not going to show up after all. Shanti gave Mira a small amount of food which she moved around her plate, picking at it as she pretended to eat. There was a continuous stream of appreciative noises as the guests polished off the food. They served themselves three, some even four, helpings.

'Wairimu and Shanti should start a catering business. Wairimu, did you hear what I just said?'

'Aiee, no, it was Shanti. I only helped her and made the paranthas. Weh, weh, we did not know our baby could cook like this.'

'Shanti, you've really outdone yourself. This is delicious.'

'Thank you. It's all because of ma, actually. They're her recipes and I cooked under her direction. And Lata aunty brought the bhajias, mutton curry and channa.'

There were tears running down Mira's face when Shanti turned to her.

'Let's have some dessert,' Shanti said, moving towards the kitchen.

While Shanti carefully spooned the strawberries into small bowls lined with silver filigree and poured the cream into a matching jug, the conversation moved on to another topic.

'So did you hear about the latest drama in parliament? This beats the time Muriuki declared that the reason Kenya Airways was doing so badly was because all the air hostesses were ugly.'

'I tell you, with politicians like ours, we are all going to hell in a hand basket.'

Shanti carried the dessert tray out into the living room, the baked strawberries were eaten without comment. She returned to Wairimu, who had brewed a carafe of coffee and boiled water for tea. She set out what was left of Mira's china coffee cups and

Lata's Japanese tea set, placing black tea and Rooibos leaves on the little silver platters Lata had lent them, and served the coffee and tea to the guests.

'It looks so pretty!' Mira suddenly exclaimed. 'It was Shanti's idea to light diyas in the spirit of Diwali, so we could celebrate hope and illumination in our house early this year.'

This would be one of the last times her mother would appreciate her own home, the house that she had made so beautiful when she cared about such things in-between her periods of depression and before she became too ill to notice.

As everyone drank their cups of coffee and tea and nibbled on wafers of After Eights, the inevitable melancholy of the occasion set in.

'I don't want to leave all of you,' Mira finally said, her voice quivering. 'This is all happening too quickly.'

Carol got up and put her arms around Mira in an uncharacteristic public display of affection.

Mohan reached over and held Mira's hand as he said gruffly, 'It will be all right.'

The emptiness of his words reverberated through the room.

Flip burst into tears and hugged Mira's legs as she rested her head against the footstool.

Lata looked entirely discomfited and her eyes frantically scanned the room as she looked for someplace comfortable upon which to fix them.

Wairimu started to clear the table.

Simon, who had hardly spoken a word the entire evening, didn't respond. He continued to lean against the stone wall as he looked steadily at Mira. His eyes were cool, his expression unperturbed. He must be used to this routine, Shanti thought. He had seen it, lived it in a variety of houses, with other people who were dying, surrounded by their grieving families.

Shanti walked out to the verandah. The air was still. The sky was thick with clouds and there were only a few lights blinking in the distance. The verandah seemed ablaze with the pale yellow flames of the diyas that lined it. Shanti couldn't help feeling that this—her mother leaving—was something she had done before, over and over. For Shanti's part, she was suddenly engulfed with a sense of remoteness that rendered her numb, as if all this were taking place behind a screen that separated her from it.

Shanti looked out into the night. The clouds had parted and she could see the city lights silhouetted against the sky, gleaming mockingly at her. They had tantalized her with the promise of a life lived with love. And then they'd taken it away, like everything else. This city had made her future uncertain, soaked in darkness, saturated in fear. The lights continued to sparkle, whispering to her, challenging her to come to terms with her place there so they could grant her wishes in the future, so she could realize her dreams at last.

What ill karma had Shanti performed that she should be plagued by these demons? Then it came to her. It was not her own karma that she was exonerating, it was her mother's.

—

Most of the guests had left when Shanti went back inside.

'Yes,' Carol was saying to Mira brightly. 'We'll be staying in a flat in central London and the IVF clinic is walking distance from there.'

'Carol, in-vitro fertilization is rarely an easy procedure,' Simon cautioned. 'This might be just the first try, or even a diagnostic test, and then you'll have to look at the alternatives you have open to you.'

'Oh, Simon, not again.' Carol rolled her eyes in exasperation. 'I've passed all the tests. And I must have spent at least a hundred hours talking to many doctors about the realistic outcomes with regard to this procedure. Believe me, my infertile world is revolving non-stop around the best and worst scenarios with IVF!'

Simon leaned forward, his eyebrows knitted with worry as he prepared to tell Carol once again not to set her expectations too high. But she raised her palm to ward off another lecture.

'Advise me all you like, Dr Lindsay, but I've done my homework,' she declared. 'I've asked all the right questions and found the right program for me. I've thought and prayed about this until my head and my heart hurt. And now I know for certain that I'm going to have a beautiful girl that will be the joy of my life!'

Shanti glanced at Simon, who was still looking troubled. Carol was almost refulgent with her faith in the procedure, and Shanti found herself unable to doubt her mother's friend's assertion that she would give birth to a daughter.

'She seems so sure, I don't think you should worry,' Shanti said to Simon. 'Call it a mother's intuition.'

'I hope you're right,' Simon conceded.

But Shanti could see that Simon, ever practical and placed squarely inside the linear realm of logic, had his misgivings.

Carol's leave-taking of Mira was joyful. Their embrace was filled with the excitement and laughter that underlay the anticipation of meeting each other once more.

'I don't even have to say goodbye to you,' Mira said to her.

'Of course you don't,' Carol agreed. 'How could you when I carry your spirit inside me?'

Mira nodded, blinking back her tears.

'I shall name her Mira after you.'

Simon offered to follow Carol to her father's home in his car. She didn't decline, it had been foolhardy of her to come by herself to begin with. After they left, the dinner party was officially over, leaving only the memories of the evening spent together wheeling around the apartment before they settled heavily like a cloud of dust, each particle glittering as bright as fireflies hovering in the dusk before a stormy night.

The teacup clattered against the saucer because Mira's hand was trembling so violently. Shanti took it from her, setting the fragile china on the table, and folded her mother's thin hands into her own. She tucked the soft razai around Mira's thin body and buried her face in the blanket. Shanti found that she was weeping. Mira held Shanti until her tears subsided. Shanti lay on the bed with her mother, nuzzling into the bony angles of her frail body until they were seamless, like two S-shaped curves that fit into each other like they were part of a jigsaw puzzle. Shanti was at once in all the rooms of the houses they had lived in, the continents where they had journeyed. She roamed through all the lives they had shared. Shanti felt as if she had returned to her mother, back into the sanctuary of her womb, where she could remain with her for ever.

23

WAIRIMU HELPED SHANTI PACK some of her belongings. They looked through postcards of Vancouver to help them decide what she should take with her. As they viewed the glossy photographs of the Canadian city—slick tarmac roads snaking through blocks of concrete, snow-covered mountains ringing the horizon—the assortment of things they had chosen for Shanti to carry dwindled to nothing.

'Ma, I have no things to take with me,' Shanti went to tell Mira, hoping that the fact that she didn't have any possessions to take to Canada would make it obvious to everyone that she couldn't possibly fit in there.

'Don't worry,' Mira said. She was sitting up and combing the thin strands of her once heavy hair. 'Your uncle will take you shopping after you arrive.'

'I don't want to go,' Shanti said. 'If I leave, I'll forget about you.'

'Darling, we'll never forget each other,' her mother said, cupping Shanti's face in her hands. 'You are a part of me, you must never forget that.'

People remembered everything, Mira explained. The mystery about leaving was not that things were forgotten, but that they weren't, so there were traces of the past turning up periodically, always being reassembled, making memories stay alive and ever changing. The biggest part of memory, she said, was desire, and where there was a desire to return to the past, there was always a potential for more memories.

But Shanti wasn't convinced. Why, lying in her mother's arms, did she believe she belonged there? There was never a real place for Shanti in Mira's life, with its distended footprint, its structure billowing out to surround her, carelessly separating her from her daughter, as it had for so many generations before. Now, despite Shanti's deepest desires, she would reap no more memories of a life that included Mira.

Mira silenced her daughter by kissing her on the mouth. It was a cloudless kiss, complete, transparent, demanding nothing in return. A kiss that in its simplicity halted Shanti's questions, arrested her pleas.

Shanti returned to her room so she and Wairimu could finish packing the few things she was taking with her. Shanti put in the two pairs of closed shoes Mira had asked Carol to buy for her from the Bata store in town while Wairimu folded the three sweaters she had.

Shanti would wear none of these things when she arrived in Canada, feeling embarrassed by the threadbare soles and bright rough wool of the items she owned.

'Mariella, can you hear me?' Shanti said again, breaking through the burst of static on the phone connection. She'd taken the cordless phone into her bedroom once she knew who was calling so late at night.

'Yes.' Mariella did not sound like herself, her voice was small and clipped.

'I missed you at the dinner party. Why didn't you come? Where are you now?'

'Kampala. We had to leave Nairobi suddenly.'

There was nothing but the sucking sounds of the ether that resided in all international phone lines. Shanti awkwardly cradled the phone between her left cheek and shoulder.

'It's my brother, Marcus. You see, he's dead.' Mariella's voice finally impaled the layers of echo that surfed across the numerous telephone grids and reached Shanti. 'He was in a car accident and they just let him die while we waited for the doctor. The nurse wouldn't help because we were Baganda. There was nothing we could do.'

'Mariella, I'm so sorry,' Shanti said. She could feel a sea of turbulence rumble deep within her. She fought to contain it but it continued to rise, sloshing messily inside her until it reached her eyes and spilled onto her cheeks.

'I have to go. I'm not supposed to talk to anyone about this,' Mariella said. 'My father doesn't want the news to get out. It's bad for politics. He's running on a platform that we are all Ugandan, our tribes do not matter.'

'Please, Mariella, write to me,' Shanti said. 'I don't know when we can see each other.'

'Okay,' Mariella replied. Shanti could hear her friend crying on the other end of the line, all by herself in a neighbouring country.

Shanti heard a series of clicks in the distance that ended the tenuous connection between them. It was only when she put down the receiver that Shanti realized her heart was beating very fast, hammering out a warning.

The night before her death, Mira lay in bed, her eyes wide and unblinking. She tried not to make any noise so she could hear the sounds that made up life around her. Mira listened to the rain outside, she imagined it soaking into the ground, reaching the roots of her rose bushes which hungrily lapped up every drop of moisture in the soil. She heard the termites that had sprouted wings in the rainfall and buzzed around the light bulbs outside. She listened to the askari creeping in during the night, after the rain had stopped, to gather the insects to eat before Wairimu had a chance to sweep them away in the morning. Mira imagined Shanti sleeping in the room next to her. She wished away her sighs of longing. She conjured images of happiness, of a love so strong that it washed over her daughter's body, rinsing her hair and rubbing into her skin.

Listen, Shanti. This is the last time I shall come to you in your dreams. It was not my intention to cause you so much pain. We have been parted from each other in so many lives, yet whenever I return to you I bring nothing but sorrow. It is not what I wanted. Soon I will turn to dust and you will have nothing of me to hold, nothing to keep. Except your memories. So hear me now before we are lost to one another once more. Hear me now so I do not fail you again. You always took my silence for hard-heartedness. How could you, my daughter who stands as strong as the sun in a world filled with shadows, believe I did not love you? Perhaps it is my fault. My silence was always intended to be a wall, a shield of love. I was silent because of my fear. I was frightened about what the truth would do to you, its awful power to scar and burn you. I was frightened it would destroy you.

I have filled your dreams with memories of my actions when I should have filled your heart with my love. I should have showed you how much I loved you. How I cherished you. Always. How I was as hungry for you as you were for me when you sucked on my breast. I was greedy for your touch, no matter how brief. I gloried in your laughter and anguished in your tears. You were—you are—my only love, my every joy. You are my heart. You are part of me.

And just see what I have gone and done. I have plagued you with these hurtful memories. I have left you with more questions than answers. Perhaps it is my fault. I loved you too much, too deeply to let you go. I have sewn myself into the fabric of your being. But it is such a dark tapestry, filled with so much sorrow.

There is so much more to tell. Had I been brave enough to speak of it, you would have seen your heritage in a different light. You would have experienced a different way of knowing me, of knowing you. Between you and me, there would have been more laughter, less silence. Your memories would be of the times we spent together, not of how we were forced to part. Had I been brave enough to speak of it, I would have begun the story—our history—with the generations that lived before us, as it always should be. For how can you know anything of yourself if you know nothing of the mothers that came before you? Those valiant women who had the courage to make decisions in the face of heartless winds bearing ill-omen—difficult decisions in the midst of tragedy, Shanti. Yes, if only I had been brave enough to speak of such painful choices, you would have seen things differently. You would have understood.

But now you come to me not seeking answers, but demanding restitution. You, with your hair so shiny and your skin so soft, your fine clothes and fancy words. You, with your quick thoughts, so ready to dismiss, so ready to judge. You, with your anger. You come searching for your story. You hunger for words to fill that great void that swallowed me and so many women before us. That dark frightening place that kept us silent.

Where can I begin, Shanti? I now realize that in so many ways you are so different from me. In so many ways, you are not me. You have so many choices, Shanti. You have the privilege of endless possibilities. In so many ways, you are still so young. How can you understand? How can you know?

The violence of my life stories reflects the histories of so many women who were trapped within the qualities of tradition. Such women remain nameless, faceless, unknown. We are powerless, enslaved by generations of silence. Our stories, if at all told, are spoken through and interpreted by men. We are the ghosts in the tales of their lives, the shadows in their stories. When we do appear, we are shown to be either goddesses or demons. When men succeeded, their victories were celebrated on our bodies; when men failed, their vengeance was played out on our bodies.

If you really want to know, you must listen with care. Look into the silence and see the stories that lie within. To truly understand, you must unravel the long pauses, the wistful sighs. Feel the weight and texture of each silence and then you will have some idea of what actually happened to each of us. You will unveil the richness of the lives and experiences that exist in mere details and trifling footnotes of the grand history of your heritage as interpreted by others. You must appreciate the value of the stories that are passed from a mother to a daughter. Look there, and you will find your answers. Look there, and you will see your face. And remember always, you were loved.

I have to leave you now, Shanti. Leave you to live your own life, find your own path. Promise me you will leave these dark dreams and walk into the dawn: your whole life awaits you there. I release you from these shadows of your mothers before. We are grateful to you. Through you, we know our stories remain, the memories of each of us live on. And take strength in the fact that the more a woman knows about the women that have been before her, the more complete she is. Go now, my sweet daughter. May I offer you my blessings, may I grant you your wishes. Because of you, my heart is filled with light, spilling outwards. Know this always.

Shanti woke in the morning, wondering at the sense of calm she felt, the cool breeze blowing against her skin.

24

IT WAS EVENING. THE lights were turned off in Mira's room, the curtains were drawn. Shanti sat in a chair close to the bed and held her mother's hand.

Mercilene gave Mira something to drink to ease her way. Shanti continued to hold her mother, preparing herself for the involuntary gasps, the violent spasms, as she let out her last breaths, fighting to live, fighting to die.

Mira was lying on her side, her hair was combed, her skin was smooth. She looked peaceful. Mira squeezed Shanti's hand; her fingers digging into Shanti's skin were the only indication that the last storms of life were passing through her.

Mira opened her mouth and spoke to Shanti. Her voice was a hoarse whisper, the words came out in staccato gasps. 'What final blessing should I leave you?'

Shanti felt Mira's thin fingers slice into her flesh as her mother conveyed how important this request was to her.

Shanti replied, her voice shaking as she heard her words resonate through the empty room, 'Bless me that I might have the courage to make the right choice, no matter how bleak my alternatives. Bless me that I might be able to give my children all that you have given me. Bless me that I might be like you, ma.'

Shanti looked into Mira's eyes, those bottomless pools of yearning, as she granted her mother her deepest wish, her heart's craving, her soul's desire. Shanti gave her mother permission to leave her. She gave her permission to die.

Winding things up in Nairobi, taking herself off the clothes hangers, neatly folding all traces and prints of her life away, packing her years into cartons and sealing it off with duct tape, turned out to be easier than Shanti had imagined. She returned the apartment they had lived in for six years to its original bare condition bar a few odd pieces of furniture. She handed over the keys to Wairimu.

It was raining the night Samuel and Wairimu drove Shanti to the airport. Raindrops glittered on the windows, denying her a last view of the city.

After saying goodbye to the only remaining people who had made up her family there, she boarded the plane. Their farewell was insufficient, the words exchanged were sparse. She knew they were lingering outside, casting a residue of worry that hovered over the threshold of the security gate. The plane took off in the middle of the vast spare land that was Africa. The sun was ascending, shedding fiery shadows on the brown plains below. Shanti knew she needed to end her thoughts of the time passed here, which were embedded in her dreams, woven into the fabric of her memories. She needed to let her memories recede into opacity. Her existence, that she kept failing, no matter how hard she tried, to make her own. Shanti could not grasp its very essence. Whenever she looked at her own life, deep into the heart of it, she saw not one but three images of herself looking back at her, and her mother stood to the side with her back turned on all three of them, her head bowed low.

Shanti learned to inhabit the instincts of a survivor, cultivating the power to invert her senses from exposure, into a hidden, protected space. She retreated into herself, moving away from anything that had the ability to hurt her. Shrinking from her exterior, she numbed her skin against elemental extremities, she muted her speech against her loneliness. Shanti would never now give cause for offence, never offer the opportunity for complaint. She would become the most quiet, most attentive student any school in the west would ever have.

Shanti found that it was easier for her to separate from her childhood if she put her memories away. She knew she should leave this part of the puzzle, especially the past shared with her mother, buried. Except the moments when Mira was happy. Those were Shanti's most treasured memories, stored away in a little cardboard box in her heart.

25

THE KITCHEN WAS ONE of her favourite rooms in the apartment, Wairimu explained to the new tenants. The window above the sink allowed you to see what the neighbours were doing, hear the latest news in the compound, all while cooking the evening meal. The tenants laughed but Wairimu couldn't see what was so funny about what she had just said. She opened a cupboard and showed them the Indian spices she'd left for them as a welcome present. She reminded them that they should mail the rent cheque to her bank in Nairobi no later than the fifth day of every month. She gave them a set of keys. Before leaving, Wairimu said again that she had paid the compound gardener extra to tend to the roses outside the master bedroom. They were important to her.

Samuel was waiting for her in the car. She had asked the retired driver to wear a uniform and a cap for the day. Wairimu got in, choosing to sit in the back. They drove upcountry.

When they arrived in Wairimu's village, a crowd gathered around the car as usual. Wairimu stepped out to greet everyone, distributing gifts and shaking the hands extended towards her. The walk to her house was slow because the heels of her pumps kept getting stuck in the soft earth. She didn't mind. The pauses allowed her to survey the village, to see if anyone was doing anything new to their houses or shambas. She stopped outside the house she had built which was now owned by her father's new wife. Wairimu had purchased two plots of land next to and behind it. There was a roller and excavator parked outside the house that she had lost, blocking its inhabitants of a view of the rest of the village. They would begin to level the land soon, in preparation for building the biggest house in the village.

When Wairimu arrived in her interim home, she remembered bringing Shanti there on the day that had accelerated if not altered her fate.

She went straight to the courtyard and sat on the chair that had been set out for her so she could begin receiving the villagers. Her daughter-in-law brought out a cup of tea for her. Wairimu mentally went over the list of projects she would need to discuss with the villagers before giving a recommendation on what they should do. There was the petition to the government to lay a pipeline from the main road to the village so everyone could have running water; the proposal to UNDP to donate a generator for which she would guarantee a safeguard. She could then charge the villagers for using it. A group of women wanted her help to get funding from the Africa Sustainability Network set up for women and youth groups, so they could put up their own petrol pump by the main road and earn revenue from that instead of farming. Then there were the minor requests and village disputes that required her counsel. It was always a very long day when she came back to her village.

After the crowds had moved away, following Wairimu through the village and to her house, Samuel got out of the car. He took off his cap and jacket and carefully placed them in the boot. He carried a bucket of water from one of the drums by the side of the road filled with the many drops they had been blessed with during this year's season of short rains. He took a small piece of cotton cloth from the glove compartment, left over from the dupatta Mira had stripped to save his hands so many years ago. Samuel wet the cloth and squeezed out the excess moisture. He started to wash his car.

Acknowledgements

A LOT OF RESEARCH went into this book. Of events, people, places and contentious weather patterns. Of history, folklore, psychology and religious beliefs. Of physical and mental states of (in)stability. Everything I read contributed to the book—especially the texts I mention here.

It is of wonder to me, who left India at age five, that I still felt compelled to write of the partition of India. It is forever part of our consciousness. Texts that had an impact here were Kushwant Singh's *Train to Pakistan* and Bapsi Sidhwa's *Cracking India*.

The real-life story of Roop Kanwar forms the basis of the sati section. Out of the numerous accounts I read, Mala Sen's *Death by Fire* provided the foundation of fact underlying the fictitious story in this book.

Growing up in Kenya, every African story I read or was told has influenced this book. The fable and song Shanti learns is adapted from Rose Mwangi's *Kikuyu Folktales*.

There are so many people to thank as well. A few in particular:

Karthika V.K., for her vision and confidence in the book.

Neelini Sarkar, for her discerning editing.

My friends from the MFA program at Warren Wilson College, for providing community, kinship and support.

My parents, for their constant love. Especially my mother, for reading so many drafts.

Tom, who appeared just in time.